Christmas in Stickleback Hollow

The Mysteries of Stickleback Hollow

By C.S. Woolley

A Mightier Than the Sword UK Publication

©2021

The Mysteries in Stickleback Hollow: Christmas in Stickleback Hollow

Christmas in Stickleback Hollow
The Mysteries of Stickleback Hollow

By C. S. Woolley

A Mightier Than the Sword UK Publication

Paperback Edition

ISBN 978-0-9951467-0-9 Paperback
ISBN 978-0-9951467-1-6 Hardback
ISBN 978-0-9951467-2-3 Epub
ISBN 978-0-9951467-3-0 Kindle
ISBN 978-0-9951467-4-7 iBook

In Loving Memory of

Oliver Henry Brown

Author's Note

Thanks for taking the time to read *Christmas in Stickleback Hollow*. I hope you enjoy it - there is much more to come in the series if you do!

At Christmas time, it can be hard for those who are away from family and friends. But even though they may be far away, they are never far from mind. Yet, we can still reach out to those who are lonely, those who cannot afford food, gifts or even to heat their homes. In this year (2021) where things have been harder than most for a few years, I hope that the Christmas spirit will be felt by all and that we do not forget those in need when stacking gifts under our own trees. Be kind, be loving and remember the lessons of the Ghost of Christmas Present (if you don't know the lessons, watch A Muppet's Christmas Carol - you won't regret it!)

The Characters

Lady Sarah Montgomery Baird Watson-Wentworth

The heroine

Bosworth

The butler

Mrs Bosworth

The housekeeper

Cooky

The cook

Mr Alexander Hunter

A huntsman and groundskeeper of Grangeback

Pattinson

An Akita, Alexander's hunting dog

Constable Arwyn Evans

Policeman in Stickleback Hollow

Doctor Jack Hales

The doctor in Stickleback Hollow

Stanley Baker

Son of Miss Baker

Lee Baker

Son of Miss Baker

Reverend Percy Butterfield

The vicar in Stickleback Hollow

Mr Thomas Egerton

Son of Wilbraham & Elizabeth

Mrs Charlotte Egerton nee Milner

Wife of Thomas

Mr Edward Christopher Egerton

Son of Wilbraham & Elizabeth

Miss Mary Pierrepont

Fiancée of Edward

Mr Richard Hales

Son of Doctor Hales

Mr Gordon Hales

Son of Doctor Hales

Miss Jessica Hales

Sister of Doctor Hales

Derwyn Evans

A welsh gentleman, brother of Arwyn, son of Edryd

Mr James Christian

A retired missionary

Mr Mitchell Claydon

An explorer

Miss Beaumont

A retired governess

Miss DeVille

A young woman of Stickleback Hollow

Mr Oliver Henry Brown

An American Gentleman, Cousin to the Egerton Family

Charlotte Egerton

Daughter of Wilbraham & Elizabeth

Captain Wilbraham Egerton

Son of Wilbraham and Elizabeth

Charles Egerton

Son of Wilbraham and Elizabeth

Sylvia

A Fallen Woman

Chapter 1

The land to which our hearts belong is often more beautiful and glorious to our eyes than any others. For Edryd Evans, there was no more divine sight, than that of his farm nestled in the hills of his beloved Wales.

The farm covered more acres than Edryd cared to count and stretched out over countless hillsides that were dotted with sheep. They had a few cows too but they were for providing milk and beef for the family. The sheep were shorn in the summer and lambs were raised until they were ready to be sold.

It was a life of peaceful contentment that was much easier without bears and wolves to steal from the flock, especially now that it was winter. The snow had fallen in a light dusting, but the truly deep snowfalls wouldn't come for a few weeks yet.

The Welshman made his way into the valley and smiled as he heard the family sound of barking. The three Welsh sheepdogs that he owned had come bounding down the lane to meet him.

There was nothing else that lay on the lane and the land on the hills on either side belonged to him. He was the king of his own private kingdom here, and it all felt so far removed from his stay at Grangeback Manor in Stickleback Hollow.

The dogs jumped and licked their master with delight and fell into step behind him as he began the final leg of his journey home. He always thought of travelling down the lane as his last leg of any journey and it allowed him to sort through all his thoughts of all that had passed whilst he had been away.

By the time the stone walls of the farmhouse came into view, he had made decisions and drawn conclusions on courses of action he wanted to take and made peace with things that had happened whilst he had been away.

The smell of chickens, cows, horses and sheep met his nostrils as he moved across the yard that lay in front of the house.

The chicken coop that provided fresh eggs every day lay to the side of the house and was right next to the kennels where the dogs slept. Any fox trying to break into the coop would have to not only come close to the house but manage to evade the three dogs as well.

Behind the chicken coop lay the cowshed and beyond that was the stable. There was a hayloft over the feed barn and a large barn that the sheep could sleep in if the weather turned bitterly cold.

At the rear of the farmhouse was a small garden with a twine washing line. His wife was stood hanging out the laundry in the yard when Edryd opened the small gate and smiled broadly at the woman he loved but had not seen in far too long.

Rather than a garden filled with flowers, the beds around the small lawn were packed with herbs of every variety as well as apple, pear and plum trees. There were gooseberry bushes and blackberry bushes as well as brambles that raspberries grew on. Strawberry plants had their own little corner of the garden and there were patches where vegetables grew alongside canes of blackcurrants.

"A fine time to arrive home!" Mrs Evans cried out as she saw her husband. There was a tinge of annoyance in her voice, but her eyes sparkled with delight, "You wait until the harvest has been done and all the preparations for winter have been made. My father always said you knew how to miss out on the hard days of work," she scolded him.

"Your father was a fine one for talking of missing hard days of work. Never did a shearing season in his life and always managed to come here the day after we needed extra hands," Edryd replied with a broad smile.

There was no malice in their conversation or in their thoughts. It was the playful teasing of a couple that felt themselves too old to say "I missed you" when they were reunited.

"I'm glad you're back safe and sound," Braith Evans said warmly as she finished hanging the laundry and moved to embrace her husband.

She was a large woman with an even larger heart, though she did have a temper that could outstrip them both if she was pushed to anger.

Edryd and Braith had spent many happy years as husband and wife, and the pair had a rhythm of life that both found to be tolerable - even if the spark of spontaneous romance had long since been extinguished.

"I'm glad to be back and see you have kept things well since I was gone. How is Gruffydd?" Edryd asked as he held his wife tightly to him.

"He's good enough, seems to have enjoyed running the farm without you breathing down his neck all the time," Braith said with a twinkle in her eye.

"Well now I'm back, there are things I need to tell you about, not all of it is good and some of it needs to be shared with all the farmhands," Edryd sighed as he let go of his wife and ran his fingers through his hair.

"What's wrong?" Braith frowned as she looked at the expression on Edryd's face.

"Don't fret, my love, it is not a problem that concerns our beloved boys. Or I should say, it is not a problem that directly concerns Arwyn. It has nothing to do with Derwyn," Edryd said, trying to dispel his wife's fears.

"Then what is it?" Braith frowned.

"Later, my dear, first, tell me all about our dear Ifanna and her Cledwyn. Then I shall tell you of Derwyn and once we have finished, then we shall deal with Arwyn," Edryd said firmly and took his wife by the elbow and steered her into the house.

The three dogs stayed out in the yard as the couple settled themselves at the kitchen table as they talked about Ifanna's life as the wife of a farmer and Derwyn's romance with Miss DeVille.

Though Edryd still did not approve of Derwyn and Miss DeVille as a pair, he was at least willing to let the young woman prove him wrong in his assessment of her.

Braith frowned for most of the conversation about Derwyn's choice of paramour, making no effort to hide that she believed he would be better finding a good Welsh girl from a farming family.

They talked for a good hour before Edryd rose for the table and went out to find Gruffydd, the farmer manager.

Gruffydd was a hard-working man, not old, but he was not young by any stretch of the imagination either. His time outside had left his skin weather-beaten with a leathery quality to it.

Gruffydd was out by the lambing field, making sure that everything was ready for the newborns that would soon be birthed by the many ewes in Edryd's flock. There was a small lambing shed that was already in use by the sheep that had given birth early and for a few of the lambs that had been rejected or left without mothers. Those lambs needed constant care.

Edryd's father had never been a man to keep those

lambs, they were too expensive to feed and hand raise too much time, but Braith had made it clear that under no circumstances was Edryd to follow in his father's footsteps. Braith had chosen to rear all those lambs that were rejected or left without mothers herself. These were lambs that were never sold for meat and became part of the permanent herd at the farm.

"I heard you were back, sir," Gruffydd said as he heard Edryd enter the shed. The man often didn't need to see anything to know it was there or who he was talking to. Often Edryd had wondered if the proud Welshman's eyesight was failing and he was using his ears to compensate, but then Gruffydd would spot one of the farmhands shirking his responsibilities from two fields away and Edryd would dismiss any concerns he had about Gruffydd's eyes.

"Not long ago. Had to speak with Braith. Derwyn's marrying an Englishwoman." Edryd replied.

"She won't be happy that she's English, but I suppose the young master knows what he is doing," Gruffydd shrugged showing he thought that Derwyn clearly did not know what he was doing.

"The Good Lord left us to make our own decisions in

life and I am not about to go against that God-given right," Edryd replied with a sigh.

"Always were a good Christian gentleman, sir," Gruffydd said with a wry smile, "I suppose you'll be wanting a report of things in your absence?"

"You can tell me about the farm and the goings-on whilst I've been away in a moment," Edryd replied, "But before you do, I have something I want you and the lads to do."

"Oh?" Gruffydd sounded surprised and looked away from the fence to his employer for the first time since his return.

"Two girls went missing, kidnapped from Stickleback Hollow whilst I was there. The police have found no trace of them, but given how close to the border they are there, the girls could have been brought here. Any oddity, no matter how small, I want us to investigate. So ears open in the pubs and listen to any gossip you can," Edryd said firmly.

"I'll make sure I tell the lads and Mrs Goggins in the post office. If those girls are here, then we'll find 'em," Gruffydd replied with sincerity.

There really is no place like home, Edryd thought and

listened as Gruffydd began to tell him every tiny detail of the happenings on the Evans farmstead.

Chapter 2

Christmas was a time of year that the Reverend Percy Butterfield rejoiced at. It was a time when people were generous, loving and gave more to cheer and merriment than they could afford during the rest of the year.

All would gather in the church and listen to his sermon each Christmas, and because of its importance, the reverend often spent weeks agonising over the contents.

The reverend believed that his sermon was supposed to inspire and uplift the congregation, and was his second favourite Christian festival after Easter.

The story of the Nativity was one that he loved to tell and one that had so much for him to explore in his sermons. So much so, even with all of his years of preaching from his pulpit, he had never once repeated himself.

Last year he had talked to his congregation about the Nativity through the eyes of King Herod and how he felt threatened by the birth of a new king.

This year Percy Butterfield had decided that he would tell the story of the Nativity through the eyes of Mary.

Though he was not a Catholic Priest, there was a great deal about Mary that made her important to the vicar.

He had always been inspired by how Mary had embraced God's plan and believed in it even though it seemed completely impossible when the angel, Gabriel, brought her the news.

It was this ideal, that nothing is impossible with God, that he had always tried to live by and a message that he could also reiterate at Easter.

He spent two hours every morning working on his sermon, then he went for a walk around the village to talk with his parishioners.

The reverend found that walking around the village not only helped him to find out what was going on in Stickleback Hollow but provided him with more opportunities to be of use to his community.

His walks had allowed him to be a practical as well as spiritual support to the people of Stickleback Hollow, and he know exactly where he was needed today.

The sun was hidden by the heavy clouds that promised snow as he walked along the road that led to the Grangeback Estate. He reached the small fork in the path, but instead of following it up towards the manor house, he veered off onto the smaller side path that lead to the groundskeeper's lodge.

Lee and Stanley Baker were stood outside the lodge, taking it in turns to beat the dust from the rugs with the giant cane rug beaters that Mrs Bosworth had given them, Pattinson, the dog, leapt between them, chasing the dust that was tossed high into the air.

The boys seemed to be having great fun trying to make the biggest dust cloud they could. The two boys had been greatly attached to Mr Hunter, who had previously resided in the lodge, but they had become especially close to Lady Sarah and the household staff of Grangeback since they had been living there for the better part of the year.

They had received an extensive education in many different aspects of life since their mother had to leave rather suddenly. They missed her greatly, but they enjoyed living at the manor. There was a lot to explore and had discovered many secrets that had been forgotten about.

As a result, they could often appear seemingly out of nowhere and often knew more about what was happening in the house than anyone else.

Bosworth, the butler, had instructed them in the duties of footmen, they had been apprenticed to the stable lads for a few weeks, Cooky had taught them about cooking, and Mrs Bosworth had taught them about housekeeping.

But it had been Mr Hunter and his duties as groundskeeper and gamekeeper that had most appealed to the two boys. They enjoyed being outside and the fun of following a man that they idolised.

But since his depression and departure from the village, the Baker boys had become quite disillusioned with the man. He had abandoned Lady Sarah and all those that had loved and supported him throughout his life.

Lee and Stanley had been disgusted that a man who they had considered to be honourable and heroic could do such a terrible thing. As a result, they had spent an increasing amount of time with Lady Sarah.

Lady Sarah had been pregnant and miscarried Mr Hunter's baby, but neither Lee nor Stanley knew anything of this. They only knew that Lady Sarah had been sick in hospital and that Mr Hunter had turned away from her.

For Lady Sarah, to have lost not only her baby, but the man she loved had been much harder on her than anyone imagined, but the almost constant presence of the Baker boys had allowed her to shower them both with love and affection and somewhat heal her broken heart.

It was due to Lady Sarah that the boys were now beating rugs outside the lodge.

Inside, Lady Sarah and Mrs Bosworth were packing away the belongings that Mr Hunter had left behind. Not only were they packing away his forgotten knick-knacks, but they were also cleaning the lodge.

This included washing all the sheets and clothes that had been left and beating the dust out of all the rugs - something that the Baker boys had leapt at the chance to try.

Two maids from Grangeback and Miss Smythe, the laundress, from Stickleback Hollow, were all hard at work on the clothing and the sheets. Three large washing tubs had been laid out behind the lodge and several washing lines had been strung up between the trees that surrounded it.

A mangle had been brought from Grangeback to help with the laundry and two scrubbing boards were being put to good use by the maids,

The reverend found Lady Sarah and Mrs Bosworth in the large of the two bedrooms at the lodge, a bedroom that had once belonged to Mr Hunter's mother and had not been changed since she died.

The two were carefully packing the clothing into wooden tea chests and descriptive labels denoting the exact contents of each chest were pasted on the lid and two sides of each chest.

Mrs Bosworth had brought plenty of mothballs to put in with each chest to protect the clothes whilst they were stored.

"There's nothing worse than getting a dress out after a season of being packed away only to find it moth-eaten and ratty," Mrs Bosworth had told Lady Sarah when she had insisted on bringing so many of them with her.

"Good morning, ladies, how goes the war on dirt?" the vicar asked jovially as he stood in the doorway of the bedroom.

"It is slow going, I'm afraid," lady Sarah replied with a sigh.

"Then tell me how I can help, and it shall be done," the vicar grinned in reply.

"The kitchen might be a good place to start. All the cupboards need emptying and everything needs to be scrubbed down," Mrs Bosworth said decisively.

"I shall wash away the dirt as Jesus washed away our sins," Percy replied and disappeared down the stairs to set about his work cleaning the kitchen.

He knew that the cupboards themselves would need cleaning, inside and out, too.

At around one o'clock, Cooky arrived at the lodge. She brought with her a large hamper filled with treats and set out a picnic outside the front of the lodge - having first taken the precaution to relieve the Baker boys of their rug beaters.

The two boys were sent to wash up before lunch as they were covered with dust and looked more like chimney sweeps than the rapscallions they were.

Everyone stopped work to eat the sandwiches, tarts, cold pies and mince pies that Cooky had brought with her. The Baker boys built a small fire, encased in the stones and the reverend found taught them how to make a spit from sticks that hung over the fire so that they could boil water.

Though it was a cold day for a picnic, the fire helped to chase away the worst of the cloud, but only reminded Mrs Bosworth that they needed to clean out the grates of each of the fireplaces.

By the end of the day, the lodge was in a much tidier state than it had begun. Though Mrs Bosworth was not entirely happy with how clean it was, it was good enough to board up in the hope that Mr Hunter would, one day, return.

The sun had long set by the time the lodge was locked and Lady Sarah led the way back to Grangeback, without a backward glance.

The reverend was invited to dinner for his help with the cleaning, and Miss Smythe had earned a week's worth of wages for a single day's work.

Lee and Stanley ran ahead of the party, and Pattinson chased after them. Lady Sarah smiled, in spite of herself, and for the first time since Mr Hunter had left, felt a glimmer of excitement about the approach of Christmas.

Chapter 3

Constable Arwyn Evans had no particularly strong feelings about the Christmas season. As he had been estranged from his family for most of his adult life, most Christmases had consisted of the traditional Christmas Day celebrations in Stickleback Hollow, but there were no gifts, no games, no Boxing Day respite from work for him.

He always enjoyed spending time with the whole village at the Grangeback Christmas feast, and it was something rather special to see the staff of the house eating side-by-side with their masters. But once the celebrations were over, he only had the lonely police house to return to and was only called upon if a crime was committed.

In the days leading up to Christmas, he was normally called away to Chester to help with the rise in alcohol-related incidents. Most of these were pub brawls that needed to be broken up as more people spent their hard-earned money on gin to mark the season or simply to keep out the ever-deepening cold.

When he returned to Stickleback Hollow, he had often

passed evenings in the company of Mr Hunter, that is since Lady Sarah had arrived in the village. The pair had become easy friends, and now that he had gone, Arwyn felt the bitter sting of betrayal and abandonment.

He knew that Lady Sarah would be feeling far worse about Mr Hunter's departure, but the pain she felt did not invalidate his own pain.

But he was by no means alone. Constable Evan's brother, Derwyn, had chosen to remain in Stickleback Hollow for the sake of a woman, but it meant that the two brothers had the opportunity to mend the broken fences that had kept them apart for so long.

Derwyn was not staying at the police house, instead, he was billeted at Grangeback, which meant that rather than sitting and drinking by the fire at the police house, his off-hours were spent in front of the drawing-room fire at Grangeback in the company of Lady Sarah, Doctor Hales, Derwyn, and Miss DeVille, Derwyn's paramour.

A note was left on the door of the police house so that anyone in need of police assistance would know where to find him.

Because he spent so much time at Grangeback in the

dark winter evenings, Constable Evans was looking forward to Christmas this year.

However, Mr Hunter was not the only member of the Grangeback household that was missing. Grace, Lady Sarah's companion, and Millie, a young woman in hiding as a charwoman, were both missing and had been for almost a year. They had gone missing just before Brigadier George Webb-Kneelingroach, Countess Szonja, Miss Baker, Mr Cartwright and Captain Jonnes-Smith had been called away on business for the crown.

No matter how long and often Arwyn and the police constables he considered to be his friends searched, there was no sign of either woman.

Their names were no longer mentioned by anyone in the village, no one wanted to think about the two girls that had seemingly vanished from under their noses.

Arwyn had not given up hope of finding them, and he knew that Lady Sarah was anxious to find out what had happened to them.

She had tried on more than one occasion to search for the two girls, but those around her had always managed to persuade her to leave the search to the hands of others.

In idle moments, Arwyn often wondered that had they let Lady Sarah search for the two women if she would have had more luck than the police. Lady Sarah had a knack for finding trouble that could often prove to be as dangerous as it was beneficial.

As Constable Evans began to ready himself for his nightly journey to the manor, there was a knock at the door. He opened it to find Constable Cantello standing on his doorstep.

"Sorry to call so late, but I need to talk to you," the constable said as Arwyn gestured for him to come in.

"Sounds like something nasty is afoot," Arwyn replied as he sat in one of the armchairs in front of his small fire grate. Constable Cantello sat in the other chair and paused to collect his thoughts before he spoke.

"Earlier today, there was an attack on a Russian diplomat. He was left badly wounded, and the man responsible for it disappeared before he could be apprehended. The suspect's name is S Kvietkus, and he was last seen on the road north towards Chester. Every policeman in every village, town and city is to be on the lookout for him."

"Is S the only clue to his name?" Arwyn asked with genuine interest,

"It is," Constable Cantello confirmed.

"I see. Is he considered to be dangerous?" Arwyn asked.

"He is, and he is likely to be armed too," Constable Cantello said seriously, "There is more you should know about the incident, but perhaps that could wait until after dinner?"

"I was going to the manor, I shall send my apologies to them and then take you to Wilson's Inn. Emma will have something hot and seasonal that we can eat. I assume you'll be staying the night?" Arwyn said with the slightest twinge of disappointment.

"With everything I have to tell you, it would be for the best if I didn't have to travel back to Chester tonight," Constable Cantello said gratefully.

"Very well," Arwyn replied and had a sinking feeling in his chest that the first Christmas he had looked forward to in a very long time was about to be ruined.

Chapter 4

Mr Alexander Hunter walked slowly along the roadside. The cold, crisp morning made the ground underfoot treacherous in places, so the former groundskeeper could only trudge slowly, his mind turning over his life in recent years.

He had always thought that once he had learned his trade as a groundskeeper from Old Mitchell, his life would be set on a steady course. There had been no plan to get married or have children, but to simply work in the great outdoors, away from the society that had shunned him all his life in the place he had felt safe and happy since he was a child.

But all that had changed when Lady Sarah had arrived at Grangeback. From the moment he had first seen her, he had loved her. He had tried to keep his distance, but she had proved his innocence and saved his life, bringing the pair closer and closer together.

He had saved her life in return, and though he had always feared that his position in life would bring ruin and shame onto the lady, he had not been able to stay away from her.

When the Brigadier George Webb-Kneelingroach, Lord of Grangeback, and guardian of Lady Sarah had revealed himself as Alex's father, and promised to recognise him as his son and heir, it had been like a dream.

Not only was he the son of a gentleman, but he could marry Lady Sarah without fear of ruining her reputation. But before he could be recognised, George had been called away - overseas, on the business of the crown.

This had left Mr Hunter as a mere groundskeeper and a scandalous pregnancy that had ended in miscarriage.

It had been one thing for Mr Hunter to face the prospect of fathering his own illegitimate child, but to lose the child before it was born, and nearly lose Lady Sarah in the process; it had been too much for him to handle.

As a result, he sank into a deep state of depression with the resolve to leave behind Grangeback, Stickleback Hollow, Lady Sarah, his father and his lost child.

He thought that leaving it all behind would be the best way to move forward, that if he was not confronted with the pain every moment of every day, then it would not trouble him as much.

Mr Hunter had known since the beginning of his relationship with Lady Sarah that it would not end well, and rather than waiting for her to leave him after losing their child, he left her first.

In his mind, it was the noble thing to do, to let the woman be free to find a better man, to be released from his love, but it did not free him of his love for her.

Nor had abandoning his home, family, and friends helped him to leave behind his pain. If anything, it had made his suffering greater, and not even wandering across the beautiful countryside of Cheshire could distract him from it.

Alex had no clear path in mind, only that he would head to the Northern Shires and find somewhere new to begin again.

As he neared the border of Lancashire, a familiar voice called out to him,

"What ho! Hunter! What the devil are you doing so far out here?" the voice belonged to Captain Wilbraham Egerton of her Majesty's armed forces.

"Sir?" Mr Hunter frowned as he stood up straighter and turned towards the source of the voice.

Captain Wilbraham Egerton was sat upon one of the

low walls and appeared to have been waiting for him. Wilbraham was the older brother of Thomas and Edward Egerton of Tatton Park, who had been childhood bullies of Mr Hunter.

One night in Chester had changed his childhood bullies from enemies to friends, and a small pocket of the upper class had received a short lesson in seeing the value in people despite the accident of their birth.

Wilbraham had not had such an awakening, but serving in the army had shown him a great deal about the nature of people and that a person's blood had very little to do with their abilities or humanity.

Mr Hunter did not know Wilbraham well, but he did know that he was well-respected by his brothers and by Lady Sarah.

"Come now, man, you know my name! I'm not your captain," Wilbraham laughed as he stood up slowly from the wall.

"I didn't know you were home, Mr Egerton," Mr Hunter replied as Wilbraham offered his hand, and Alex tentatively shook it.

"Dear God in heaven, Hunter, there is no one else

around for miles, call me Wilbraham! No one will ever know," the captain shook his head and slapped Alex on the back with affection.

"Why were you here waiting for me, Wilbraham?" Alex asked with discomfort.

"The rumour mill has been churning, and to listen to Charlotte and Mary, one would think that the witch had driven you away from your home. So I thought I might find you and tag along for a tour of the homeland before I leave it once more," Wilbraham replied jovially as he began to make his way down the road, motioning for Mr Hunter to fall into step beside him as he went.

"It is not so far from the truth, though perhaps it would be best not to inform the ladies of that," Alex replied with a shake of his head.

"I know, or at least I surmised as much. I went to visit Lady Sarah after the business with the hospital. Thomas and Edward told me all about your adventures since I last saw you all at the All Hallows' Eve Ball, my God, more than a year ago! I wanted to know if those tales had been exaggerated, but I feel that my brothers only knew a small amount of what actually happened," Wilbraham sighed, and shook his head.

"That is true, though you would not want to know all the intimate details of recent events," Mr Hunter replied with a grunt.

"Though you may find it hard to believe, I may know more than you think. Your mother, God rest her, she was a great friend of mine. I know that you didn't know I knew her, and it was a chaste relationship. I have always found it hard to talk to women, but your mother and Lady Sarah both put me at great ease. They both share a warm quality that makes one feel as though you could tell them anything. Your mother would often visit Tatton Park with the brigadier's wife and be left to sit and wait whilst my mother and the brigadier's wife did whatever it is that ladies do when they saw one another regularly," Wilbraham sighed and took a deep breath before he continued.

"It left a great deal of time for me to talk to with her. We became good friends, just before I left for the army, she confided in me about your parentage. I think she felt guilty that after we had been so honest and close that she was holding something back."

"What were you to my mother?" Mr Hunter asked

with a furious look on his face.

"A confident and friend. Oh, Hunter, would it set your mind at ease if I told you that I confided in her in return?" Wilbraham asked with a wry smile.

"Confided what?" Alex asked with slight confusion.

"That I have always preferred the company of men and that I am not the type of man to ever take a wife or any other form of woman," Wilbraham replied flatly.

Mr Hunter did not know what to say as he processed what Wilbraham had told him.

"You have no interest in women?" Alex finally asked.

"None at all, though I also have found that there are very few men that I am attracted to, so perhaps I am attracted to neither and am much happier being friends with those that I find to be worthwhile," Wilbraham shrugged, "There was nothing that I could hold back from your mother, and the same is true of Lady Sarah. We have been corresponding since we first met. I think it started as a way of her coping with her homesickness, but after a time, she seemed to forget to ask about the land she once called home."

"There was a great deal she said that could not be written of in letters, but when I called on her, she told me everything that had transpired and I am truly sorry for you both," Wilbraham said quietly.

"I see, thank you," Mr Hunter replied and gritted his teeth as he fought to control the emotions that welled up inside of his chest.

"I mean it. You made a handsome pair, and one that even my brothers have been hoping to see together - and as you know, it is not like Thomas or Edward to talk of couples or good matches," Wilbraham chuckled. Mr Hunter smiled, in spite of himself, as he imagined Thomas and Edward clucking like old hens about such a thing.

"It would have been such a gift to see the two of you together with a child. Do not fear though, I will not tell anyone about any of this. But I felt that your choice to leave was one made out of pain, and a man should never have to bear such a burden alone, so though you may wish to be walk and tramp as a single vessel tossed on a lonely sea, I cannot allow it, I am your companion for the road, no matter where it might lead us. You can choose to talk or choose to keep your thoughts and feelings to yourself. But no matter what, you have a companion to share this green and pleasant land with," Wilbraham explained, and Mr Hunter nodded.

Wilbraham's presence, though unwanted, was a great comfort, and Mr Hunter was glad to have the kindly captain to share the road with.

"It is for the best," was all Alex said.

"Perhaps, but I have almost always found that whenever someone says that, the opposite is true," Wilbraham replied and before Alex could reply, Wilbraham began to whistle Christmas Carols.

Chapter 5

With the lodge cleaned and Mr Hunter's belongings stored, the preparations for Christmas at Grangeback Manor could begin in earnest.

With the brigadier absent this year, there was much that Lady Sarah had to organise, and she was glad to have the help of Derwyn and Miss DeVille.

Not only did the decorating need to be overseen, but the menu for Christmas Day needed to be approved, and the gifts for all those who would be attending the Christmas dinner needed to be bought.

There were lots of gifts that the brigadier was in charge of procuring every year, and Lady Sarah was worried that she would not be able to rise to the challenge of not only providing the gifts but providing gifts that were as thoughtful as the ones that the brigadier would buy.

Mrs Bosworth knew how the house needed to be decorated, and needed very little input from Lady Sarah in order to create the Christmas atmosphere that would set the mood for the feast on Christmas Day.

Each room had a specific design that had been perfected over many years of decoration. For most of the rooms, there were elaborate nativity scenes that had been specially crafted for the family. There were great wreaths and festive floral arrangements that were created from dried flowers and fresh foliage.

On Christmas Eve, Mrs Bosworth had all of the maids brought together to make the final decorations for the tables for the feast so that they would have the greatest impact on their guests.

The footmen, under the direction of Bosworth, the butler, were responsible for setting out the tables, chairs and laying each place at the table. Bosworth needed no instruction in his duties and had already begun the painstaking process of polishing all the silverware and glassware for the feast.

Cooky had spent many years cooking the Christmas feast for Christmas Day at Grangeback and was able to create the menu that simply needed a nod from Lady Sarah.

There were five courses that needed to be planned and prepared for the whole village, something that was a mammoth operation, but a challenge that Cooky was always happy to attack with all of her skills and energy.

The kitchen staff began working on the meal after dinner on Christmas Eve had been cleared away. They worked until 3 o'clock in the morning, were allowed to sleep for four hours, and then were expected to be back at their stations at 7 o'clock.

Cooky never slept on Christmas Eve, instead, she, Bosworth and Mrs Bosworth would take care of all the tasks around the house that the maids and footmen had not been able to complete before they went to bed.

Once they had been completed, Cooky would prepare the meats so that when the kitchen staff were awake, they could begin cooking.

Spits over open fires were set up in the courtyard outside the kitchen door so that the roast hog and mutton could be cooked through slowly along with the chickens. Inside the kitchen, the geese and turkeys were roasted, the vegetables and potatoes were cooked, the soup was boiled, the puddings were steamed and the meals were plated up onto giant platters so that the footmen could carry them out to the tables once they were ready.

It was an elaborate and extensive operation that never

failed to bring joy to the village after the Reverend Percy Butterfield had finished his sermon.

The household ran like a well-oiled machine that needed very little maintenance. This allowed Lady Sarah to focus all of her attention on the gifts. After spending a few days wandering around all of the shops in Stickleback Hollow, it had become clear to the young lady that she would need to look further afield for the perfect presents for Christmas Day.

But there were so many gifts to buy, she could not possibly hope to find them all alone. So she enlisted the help of the Baker boys, Derwyn and Miss DeVille. The Baker boys knew the streets of Chester like the back of their hands, Derwyn had the bartering skills that came from a lifetime of trading at markets, and Miss DeVille had flawless taste.

With only six days to go until Christmas Day, Lady Sarah, Lee Baker, Stanley Baker, Derwyn Evans and Miss DeVille all climbing into the larger of the brigadier's carriages and made their way to Chester.

Chapter 6

The journey to Chester was uneventful, though Derwyn learned a lesson about travelling with adolescent boys, and marvelled at how the Baker boys knew exactly how far they could push their luck with him.

More than once on their journey, Derwyn had thought to himself, *Just one more word and I'll throw these boys out of this coach.* But neither boy would cross that line until long after frustration had passed Mr Evans by.

To Lady Sarah, Lee and Stanley were a great comfort and rarely did anything to irritate her. Miss DeVille felt sorry for Derwyn, as it was clear that the two boys had become fixated on him in Mr Hunter's absence, and, unlike the groundskeeper, the farmer did not have the ability to handle the boys.

As they reached the city walls, Lee Baker leant out of the carriage window and shouted something to the driver. No one in the carriage could hear what he said, but the carriage slowed and lurched left as it trundled into the heart of Chester.

The carriage stopped outside a store that Lady Sarah had not visited before, but she was certain that it was the first place that Lee and Stanley Baker wanted to visit.

The store was one of the largest confectionery shops in the North of England, and it was rare that the Baker boys could afford to buy much from there.

Lady Sarah had promised the two boys that they could choose some treats for the feast before they had left for Chester, and now the two boys were prepared to make some a lot.

In the sweet shop, there were huge glass jars that were filled with all manner of treats, trays of exotic delicacies and a jolly shopkeeper who was ready to serve with a smile and recommendations of more that could be bought.

By the time the boys were through with making selections, Lady Sarah had bought at least a quarter of all the store's stock. There were boxes and parcels that Derwyn and the Baker boys ferried out to the carriage to stow safely inside.

Whilst the boys were outside, Lady Sarah took the opportunity to purchase a few treats that would just be for the Baker boys to enjoy, making sure that they were hidden by the time the two boys came back into the shop.

Miss DeVille and Derwyn had their own shopping to do, so took the opportunity to shop for themselves, arranging to meet Lady Sarah and the Baker boys for lunch at one of the tea rooms.

Lee and Stanley walked one ahead and one behind Lady Sarah along the pavement, making sure that any cutpurses were warded off and that the young lady was kept safe from anyone that might do her harm.

The two boys had vivid memories of the attempt that was made to kidnap Millie and Grace when shopping in Chester, and both were determined that nothing like that would ever happen again.

As they made their way through the city streets, and stopped in at stores to purchase everything from mittens, gloves and scarves to books, sweet meats and even jewellery. There was far too much for Lady Sarah and the boys to carry, but the carriage followed them down the street and the coachman was happy to guard all the gifts as they piled up inside.

When the interior, trunk and roof had been piled high with presents, the coachman had left the city to deliver the packages to Grangeback. Once the carriage was empty, he would return to the city for the rest of the shopping and his passengers.

The clock on the Cathedral struck 12, so Lady Sarah and the Baker boys turned away from the shops and made their way towards the tearoom.

There streets of Chester were full of people, some were shoppers making their way about, preparing for their own Christmas celebrations, others were picking pockets, and then there were those begging for any change that they could scrounge.

Though Lee and Stanley kept the pickpockets at bay, those that were begging were harder to keep from Lady Sarah. She felt a great compassion for those who slept on the streets, especially during the cold of the winter months.

Whenever she was on the streets of a city, whether in England or India, she always made sure that she had coins that she could give to those in need.

There always seemed to be more hands than coins in the bigger cities, but in Chester, Lady Sarah normally had enough coins for those that held out a hand as she passed.

Lee and Stanley Baker stuck close to Lady Sarah as

she handed out the silver coins to those who begged along the side of the street., making sure that no one got too close to her.

As the coins began to dwindle, Lady Sarah spotted a familiar figure huddled on the ground, with her hand extended.

"Sylvia?" Lady Sarah asked tentatively as she stood before the hunched woman. Her clothes were torn, and her skin was pale, but Lady Sarah was sure that it was the same woman she had befriended during her captivity at Duffleton Hall.

"You? What do you want?" Sylvia asked, first with surprise, and then with mistrust.

"I am Christmas shopping. May I introduce Lee and Stanley Baker," Lady Sarah said as she pointed to each of the boys in turn.

"Must be nice," Sylvia said and cast her head back to the floor.

"What happened to you?" Lady Sarah asked with concern.

"What I knew would happen. I'm a fallen woman, no respectable person will have anything to do with me," Sylvia spat bitterly.

"That isn't true at all. I would be honoured if you would care to help the boys and myself with our shopping, and with all of the preparations I still need to make at the manor. Our friends have deserted us and I find we are in need of another woman's eye," Lady Sarah said kindly.

"And what interest would I have in shopping with someone like you?" Sylvia asked with narrowed eyes. Lee and Stanley Baker bridled at her tone, but stayed silent whilst Lady Sarah spoke,

"Some new and warm clothes to help you through the winter months and I would pay you for your valuable time," Lady Sarah replied thoughtfully.

Sylvia didn't know what to say as she looked up at Lady Sarah. In her eyes, Lady Sarah could read the inner battle that was being fought in Sylvia's mind between her pride and her immediate need for new clothes and food.

It was her need that won out in the end, and she slowly rose to her feet and meekly followed Lady Sarah to the closest seamstresses shop.

"Well boys, find me all a lady needs for winter," Lady Sarah instructed the Baker boys as they stepped through the door, and the two boys rushed about the store picking things and issuing instructions to the seamstress, who looked more than a little taken aback.

"Why would you send two boys to find clothes for me?" Sylvia frowned as she rubbed her cold arm with her numb fingers.

"They are the sons of my seamstress in Stickleback Hollow and know more about clothes than anyone I know. I doubt that anyone could find you more perfect clothes than they. Especially as they have no concept of money yet, not really," Lady Sarah grinned.

When the two boys had finished, there were more clothes than Sylvia had ever owned in her life piled on the counter.

The two boys chose a dress, cloak, stole and gloves, whilst Lady Sarah chose the underwear. Sylvia was then ushered off to change into them, and given a bowl of warm water to wash with before she put the clothes on.

The rest of the clothes were wrapped in brown paper and the seamstress agreed to send them to Grangeback on the lady's behalf.

When Sylvia emerged from the backroom, her face

shone, though her hair was still damp. The dress fitted her as though it had been made for her and it was clear that she no longer felt the cold as she had in her rags.

Stanley Baker shyly offered her a bonnet to cover her wet hair and keep out the wind and the outfit was complete.

"Now, I believe it is time for lunch," Lady Sarah announced, and led her companions towards the tea rooms once more.

As they made their way down the street, a voice called out from a carriage,

"Lady Sarah! What a pleasure!" the carriage door swung open and out of it leapt Edward and Thomas Egerton, with their cousin, Mr Oliver Henry Brown.

"Edward, Thomas, it seems I can hardly go anywhere without seeing you these days," Lady Sarah teased the two men, who grinned at her in reply.

"Your Ladyship, it is an honour to see you again," Mr Brown drawled in his thick American accent, and bowed low.

"The honour is mine, Mr Brown, how are you finding England?" Lady Sarah asked as she offer a slight curtsey to the visiting gentleman.

"Cold, and different, but I have been promised a truly memorable Christmas," Mr Brown replied, as he rubbed his hands together, "And who are your companions?"

"I am sure you will have seen Master Lee Baker and Master Stanley Baker running wild at the manor, they my wards for the most part, but today, they are my bodyguards. This charming lady is Miss Sylvia," Lady Sarah said, covering easily the fact that she did not know Sylvia's surname.

"Miss Sylvia must be your new lady's maid. It has been a long time since, well, I, what a pleasure to meet you," Thomas stammered as Edward elbowed him in the ribs.

"Miss Sylvia, may I introduce to you Mr Thomas Egerton, Mr Edward Egerton, and Mr Oliver Henry Brown, all of Tatton Park, Mr Brown by way of the Americas," Lady Sarah said warmly.

"Such beautiful women in every aspect of society here," Mr Brown smiled at Sylvia, who arched her eyebrow in response, "My apologies, I didn't mean to offend," Mr Brown said hurriedly when he noticed Sylvia's expression.

"Miss Sylvia is not one for empty flattery," Lady Sarah said with mild amusement.

"Then I shall only engage in sincere flattery from now on," Mr Brown replied with a bow.

"I am glad that we have seen you today, Mother was sending us to Grangeback to invite you and your guests to join us at Tatton Park for Christmas Eve," Edward said, preventing Oliver from offering more compliments to the ladies.

"We would be delighted, but only if your family and guests would agree to join us at Grangeback for Christmas Day," Lady Sarah replied.

"I am sure that will delight not only the family but the servants as well," Thomas laughed.

"We must beg to take our leave now, we are meeting Mr Evans and Miss DeVille for lunch at the tea rooms, and I fear we have kept them waiting for far too long," Lady Sarah said apologetically.

"Ah, alas, such a short, but sweet meeting," Mr Brown smiled.

"Until Christmas Eve then!" Thomas said and ushered his cousin and brother back into the carriage.

"Goodbye," Sylvia said politely.

The carriage lurched away and the three men waved

out of the carriage windows until they became lost in the traffic of the city.

"Why did you not correct them when they asked if I was your maid?" Sylvia asked with a frown.

"Perhaps it is because I was going to offer you the job once you had spent a few days at the manor," Lady Sarah shrugged.

"I, I don't know what to say," Sylvia sounded astonished as she spoke.

"I hoped that you would say yes," Lady Sarah replied, "But I will wait for a few days to ask you so that you have time to think on it. Now, we are terribly late for lunch."

Chapter 7

The rest of the day in Chester passed far quicker than Lee and Stanley Baker imagined it would. More packages had been purchased, in fact, there were so many that a second carriage had to be hired to carry all the gifts and passengers back to Grangeback.

It was dark by the time the carriages pulled up outside the manor and Mrs Bosworth led out a contingent of maids and footmen to collect all the parcels and packages from inside.

"Welcome home, my lady," Bosworth said as he helped the young lady out of the carriage.

"Thank you, Bosworth, I hope Cooky isn't too cross that we are so late," Lady Sarah replied with a smile.

"Not in the least, she thought you might be home a little later than usual. Doctor Hales is also a little late too, his sons are joining us for dinner as well. They have returned home for Christmas, though they have elected to stay at Doctor Hales home instead of in the guest rooms here," Bosworth informed the lady.

"I am looking forward to seeing them both again. Now I have a guest to introduce to you. This is Sylvia, she is staying with us for a few weeks as my lady's maid, to help with all the Christmas preparations," Lady Sarah said as Sylvia followed Derwyn and Miss DeVille out of the carriage.

"I will ensure that Mrs Bosworth has rooms prepared for her and introduce her to the staff after dinner. I will also inform Cooky that there will be another place for dinner," Bosworth bowed slightly to Sylvia, his face a passive mask that betrayed no emotion or opinion at the news of a new addition to the household.

"This is where you live?" Sylvia asked, her mouth hanging open slightly as she took in the whole house.

"It is. It belongs to Brigadier George Webb-Kneelingroach, my guardian. He is currently out of the country, so all the Christmas traditions have fallen to me this year - which is why I need your help," Lady Sarah explained as she led the way into the house.

"Mrs Bosworth, could you show the house to Sylvia, please? I have some gifts to wrap whilst the Baker boys beg Cooky for some treats before dinner," the young lady asked of the housekeeper as she stepped into the hall and removed her cloak, bonnet and gloves.

"Of course, your ladyship. Miss DeVille and Mr Evans, drinks will be served in the drawing room as soon as Bosworth has finished with the parcels," Mrs Bosworth said and motioned for Sylvia to follow her.

The parcels and packages that had been bought in Chester and Stickleback Hollow had all been taken to the ballroom. The ballroom would be where the great feast would be held on Christmas Day as it was the only room that was big enough for all of the people from Stickleback Hollow, the household staff of Grangeback, and the other guests that had been invited.

Not only would the ballroom be filled with people but all the gifts too.

It would take days of work to prepare the ballroom for the feast and wrap all of the gifts. Parcel paper lay in piles in the corner of the room, along with rolls of string.

The thought of all the work was overwhelming to the young lady, and Sylvia agreeing to help her with all the preparations had been a great relief.

As she searched through the packages to find the two small boxes of treats that she had purchased for the Baker boys.

It did not take her long to cut the brown paper and careful wrap each of the boxes, then tie them with string. She then wrote Stanley and Lee's names on two slips of paper and tucked them under the string.

These were not the first Christmas gifts to be wrapped, those that had been wrapped, were placed on the sideboards and tables that lined the walls of the room. Normally these would be used to rest drinks upon or serve punch from, but over Christmas they were loaded with gifts for all the guests that were expected.

The gifts for the household would be placed in the drawing room for Boxing Day when the staff would receive their gifts from the brigadier and Lady Sarah. The gifts for the guests of the house and Lady Sarah were kept in the front parlour and opened after the household staff had opened theirs and left to celebrate their seasonal day off.

For the moment, the tables around the edges of the room were being used for all the gifts, and the piles would be moved to the parlour and drawing room when the banquet tables were being laid.

Lady Sarah smiled to herself as she placed the two

wrapped boxes on the table and thought of the surprise that the boys would have on Boxing Day. The door to the ballroom opened and closed as Mrs Bosworth joined Lady Sarah.

"Cooky is ready to serve dinner as soon as you are, my lady," Mrs Bosworth announced as she surveyed all that Lady Sarah had bought for Christmas.

"I think I may have to go to Manchester for the other gifts," Lady Sarah sighed as turned and shook her head.

"Surely there is more than enough here!" Mrs Bosworth exclaimed.

"Not quite, there are a few things that I couldn't find. There are also some things for the feast that I want to try to find," Lady Sarah replied as she chewed her bottom lip in thought.

"Though I admire your Christmas Spirit, you do not need to do more than you already have. Those coming will be delighted with all you have done, and it is surely better that we are all able to celebrate together," Mrs Bosworth replied.

"Only we are not all together. Until the brigadier, Mr Cartwright, Mr Hunter and Miss Baker are home, we will not all be together," Lady Sarah surprised herself as much as Mrs Bosworth with her sudden outburst, "I am sorry, Mrs Bosworth, I did not mean to - I apologise."

"You have done more to make Christmas a time of joy in this village than anyone would have ever dreamed of. Lee and Stanley Baker both miss their mother, but they love you dearly and I know that it means so much to them to be here and part of these preparations," Mrs Bosworth said gently.

"Thank you, Mrs Bosworth. Perhaps I am overtired, it has been a long day. As long as Doctor Hales has arrived with his sons, tell Cooky that I am ready for dinner to be served," Lady Sarah replied with a pained smile.

Mrs Bosworth nodded and left Lady Sarah in the ballroom. A few moments later, the dinner gong sounded and Lady Sarah took a deep breath before she made her way to the dining room.

Sylvia was stood in the dining room looking slightly lost. Lee and Stanley Baker bolted into the room behind Lady Sarah and rushed to their places at the table.

"Good evening, Lady Sarah, you remember my sons, Richard and Gordon," Doctor Jack Hales said as he entered the room, flanked by his two sons.

"Why of course, good evening to you all. It is wonderful to see you both again. May I introduce Miss Sylvia. Sylvia this is Doctor Jack Hales, Richard Hales and Gordon Hales. Miss Sylvia is here to assist me with the preparations for Christmas and may choose to stay as my lady's maid," Lady Sarah explained amidst the introductions.

The moment Lady Sarah had finished, Gordon's face was filled with a thunder.

"You are giving up then?" he demanded coldly.

"Giving up?" Jack frowned at his son.

"On Millie and Grace, you are replacing Grace with this woman, so you must be giving up!" Gordon cried.

"Mr Hales, though I understand your distress, there is no reason for you to raise your voice to a woman in her own home," Derwyn announced from behind the doctor.

"And who are you sir?" Gordon sneered.

"This is Mr Derwyn Evans, Edryd's son and Arwyn's brother. He is a guest in this house, and beside him is his fiancée, Miss DeVille," Doctor Hales explained.

"And what do you understand of my distress, sir?" Gordon asked icily, ignoring his father's introductions.

"There is not a soul in this village who does not

lament the disappearance of the two young ladies you referred to. But Miss Sylvia is not responsible for their absence, neither is Lady Sarah, and there is no excuse for such rude behaviour towards either of them," Derwyn replied emphatically.

"Please gentlemen, this is not a season for ill feeling. Miss Sylvia is here to help me during this time, and even if she did want to take the position as my lady's maid, Grace would still be welcomed back to Grangeback once she has been found. As will Millie," Lady Sarah replied.

Gordon snorted in reply, but for the moment, he seemed satisfied not to push the issue any further.

The gentlemen and Miss DeVille took their seats at the table, though Sylvia hung back, uncertain of whether it would better to dine with the others, or retreat to her room until Gordon Hales had left.

"Please, Sylvia, come sit beside me," Lady Sarah said, gently taking her by the arm and leading her to the table.

"I don't understand -" Sylvia began.

"I will explain all after dinner, there is a lot you should know, especially if you do want to be my companion," Lady Sarah replied in whisper, but assured

Sylvia with a smile before they sat down and Cooky sent out the dinner.

Chapter 8

After Constable Cantello had departed the morning after his unexpected visit, Constable Arwyn Evans was feeling somewhat deflated. In order to try and find some Christmas spirit and to check the village for any signs of S Kvietkus.

As he stepped out into the cold, the smell of burning wood on the crisp winter air made him feel better than he had the night before. He was about to set off on a tour of the village, when he noticed the Reverend Percy Butterfield hurrying down the road towards him.

"Good morning, reverend, whatever is the matter?" Arwyn asked with a slight frown.

"Please, constable, I need you to come with me," the vicar said with a measure of alarm.

"What on earth is wrong?" the constable asked as he carefully made his way out onto the road, deftly avoiding the patches of ice that were hidden by the snowfall.

"There's a man in the graveyard, please, you need to come," the reverend said and set off at a brisk pace.

It was odd to think of an aged man like Percy Butterfield moving so quickly that it was difficult for the policeman to keep up with him, but he easily outstripped Arwyn, leaving the constable jogging to try and keep up.

The problem with jogging in the winter weather conditions is that there was a great risk of the constable slipping and falling. Whether by luck or Divine Providence, the policeman managed to keep his feet and reached the graveyard only a few steps behind the reverend, though very much out of breath.

The graveyard looked beautiful and unspoilt, aside from one set of footprints that led across it from the vicarage.

"Where is this man?" Arwyn frowned as he looked around for another living soul.

"Over here, by the verger's grave," the vicar beckoned and showed the constable one of the newer headstones in the graveyard that a man was slumped against.

The man's skin was devoid of colour and his eyes were wide and staring. His shirt was soaked in blood and it was clear that he had been dead for sometime.

"Did you walk home through the graveyard last night?" Constable Evans asked.

"Yes, there was nothing amiss then, the man definitely wasn't there," the vicar replied.

"Did you hear anything last night?" Arwyn asked as he crouched beside the body.

"Not a peep, I'm afraid, though, I took my sleeping powders just after 9 o'clock and would only have been woken by the rapture," the reverend said with disappointment.

"I need to send for help from Chester, if I am right, this man is well-known to them and he might have just ruined my Christmas," Arwyn sighed.

"What should I do?" the vicar asked.

"Make sure no one comes into the graveyard. I will be back as soon as I can," Arwyn replied as he turned on his heel and jogged back towards the police station.

Chapter 9

It only took a few hours for Constable Cantello to arrive from Chester along with Constables Clowes, McIntyre and McGill. They were also accompanied by a senior officer that Arwyn did not know and did not take the time to introduce himself to the lowly constable.

"Is it him?" Arwyn asked Constable Cantello in a hushed voice as the senior officer conversed with the Reverend Percy Butterfield.

"It looks that way, and with all that blood on his shirt, his death can't have been an accident," Constable Cantello replied in equally hushed tones.

"Who is the overseer?" Arwyn asked as he nodded his head in the direction of the senior officer.

"That? He's the nephew of Captain Jonnes-Smith, though he seems to throw his uncle's name around a lot, word is that the Superintendent isn't overly fond of him and he's only part of the force because the Chief Constable's sister insisted," Constable Cantello replied, "Since the captain's been away, he's been much worse than normal. Always saying what his uncle would want or think."

"Does Napoleon have a name?" Arwyn asked dryly.

"Inspector Bracey, so you can imagine some of the nicknames that the sergeants have, let alone us rank and file," Constable Cantello grinned.

"Watch out, the emperor wants us all," Constable McIntyre hissed as he joined the two men. The three all looked in the direction of Inspector Bracey who was waving for all the constables to attend him in a rather ridiculous manner.

"Caesar calls," Constable Clowes said dryly as he joined the others and they made their way over to where the inspector was. The only one who didn't move was Constable McGill, who stood guarding the entrance to the graveyard.

"Though we cannot say without a friend or relative stating positively that this is S Kvietkus, we can reasonably assume that this man is him," Bracey announced in a voice that was far louder than it needed to be.

"And that he was murdered, sir?" Constable Clowes asked as innocently as he could.

"Well, we can't assume that either. No, there will have to be an investigation, and the coroner will need to be called," Inspector Bracey replied, his chin tilted in the air and his face etched in lines that indicated deep thought.

It took all the self-control that the constables possessed to keep them from bursting into laughter.

"Then let me investigate here, sir," Arwyn volunteered, "and you can return with the body to Chester, oversee thinks from the city," the constable tried to sound sincere as he spoke.

"Quite right, Constables McIntyre and Cantello will stay here to guard the body until the coroner arrives. Constables McGill and Clowes will come back to Chester with me. Constable Evans, you will start your investigation here and will report everything you find to me, in person," Inspector Bracey instructed.

"Yes, sir," the constables chorused.

"Well then, get about it men," Inspector Bracey said with mild irritation.

"Don't worry, the reverend will make sure you get plenty of Christmas cheer," Arwyn winked at Constables Cantello and McIntyre.

"What kind of Christmas cheer?" Constable McIntyre asked.

"At least 70 proof," Arwyn grinned in reply and set about examining the scene.

There was very little evidence that could be seen, the snow had covered any possible footprints and as there were no footprints in the snow it was impossible to know whether the man had been attacked in the graveyard or had stumbled his way towards the church after he had been attacked.

"Reverend, I am going to need your spade," Arwyn sighed. The only way he would find out was to dig through the snow and hope that it hid some clues.

Chapter 10

The policemen had to stand out all night in the snow whilst they waited for the coroner to arrive. Arwyn did not have to stand guard, and after he had searched through as much of the snow as he could and found no evidence whatsoever, the constable of Stickleback Hollow made his way home to the police house.

As he opened the door to the police house, he saw a letter lying on his door mat. It was an unassuming looking letter and Arwyn recognised the handwriting as that of his father.

He knew that he did not have long before he would need to leave the warmth of the police house and make his way back through the cold night to join his friends for dinner at Grangeback, but there was just enough time for him to sit and enjoy a cup of tea whilst he read his father's missive.

The fire in the large kitchen grate was never allowed to go out during the day. It warmed the house and allowed the young policeman to cook and boil the kettle in very short order.

During the night hours, the thick blankets piled on his bed and the hot embers that glowed through the night were all he had to keep warm.

He never left a fire burning in any of the grates at night for fear of the fire spreading to the house and engulfing him whilst he slept.

Though at night the house was cold outside of his blankets, but right now it was warm, so, after he had removed his cloak, he settled down in his chair in front of the fire and opened the letter from his father.

My dear son,

I hope that your brother is behaving himself at Grangeback, and that Miss DeVille continues to make him happy. Your mother is as thrilled with the news as we expected, though less than enamoured with the idea of an English daughter-in-law.

I will always be grateful for the time we were able to spend together in Stickleback Hollow, and hope that we will be able to welcome you at the farm soon.

Though I know that a visit to Wales will have to wait

in light of what we have found. Since I returned home, the lads on the farm and I have all been searching for news of your missing women. I have sent a messenger who will tell you all that we have found. I hope that he will reach you soon. He had business in one of the cities but assured me he would not delay in bringing you what we know.

I sincerely hope that what he has to say will lead you to your missing women before the new year begins.

His name is S Kvietkus. He has spent a number of months working for our family in Wales, and has proven to be useful, even for a foreigner. I would not send him to you if I did not trust him.

Until we meet again

Your father,
Edryd

Arwyn read the letter four times with disbelief. After the fourth reading, he put the letter to one side and sat back in his chair with his fingers steepled.

The only information about the possible whereabouts

of Grace and Millie had died along with S Kvietkus in the graveyard of Stickleback Hollow.

Though Arwyn knew that they cold journey to Wales to find out what his father knew first hand, the constable would be unable to leave until after S Kvietkus' murder investigation was complete.

Not only that, but the investigation would only be more complicated now. He sighed deeply whilst he considered the best course of action. He could withhold information his father had sent him in the letter, but if Edryd had also written to Derwyn, then it would not be long before Lady Sarah involved herself in the investigation, and without Mr Hunter there to help her, Arwyn knew that he needed to be able to keep an eye on her.

He shook his head and cursed before he got to his feet, picked up the letter. Making sure the fire was contained in the grate, he left it to burn out as he picked up his cloak and made his way out into the night.

The bitter cold of the evening was now tinged with rain. A light rain that soaked everything it fell upon and soon permeated through the heavy police coat.

By the time Arwyn had walked from the village to the

Grangeback estate, he was so cold and wet that his mood had turned foul.

Bosworth opened the door and welcomed the constable warmly, but the chilly response made the butler take Arwyn by the arm and escort him, wet cloak and all, into the bustling warmth of the kitchen.

"Constable Evans, what a frightful night it is, come, come, the fire is hot and there is a pot of tea on," Cooky clucked. Cooky was a jolly woman, whose demeanour only grew more jovial the closer Christmas became.

Bosworth removed the wet cloak from Arwyn's shoulders in a smooth motion, careful not to flung water all across the kitchen as he did so.

Cooky seized Arwyn by the hand and plonked him in one of the wooden country chairs that sat by the large hearth in the kitchen.

Bosworth disappeared from the kitchen and moments later, Mrs Bosworth appeared with a pile of dry clothes in her arms.

"Drink this, nice and hot," Cooky instructed firmly, forcing a mug of warm tea into his hands, before she turned around to yell at one of the scullery maids, who had stopped stirring the soup.

"As soon as you've finished that, you can change into these. There from the Brigadier's wardrobe. He's not worn them since he was a young man in his twenties, so he won' miss them," Mrs Bosworth instructed. Her eyebrow arched as she spoke, clearly disapproving of Arwyn walking so far in the rain without an umbrella.

Arwyn didn't say a word, but he did as both Cooky and Mrs Bosworth instructed. He knew better than to argue with the two women. Once the tea was drunk, he nodded his thanks to the cook and followed Mrs Bosworth to one of the disused rooms of the west wing so that he could change in private.

The room Mrs Bosworth showed him to had a fire lit and a clothes horse had been set up in front of the fire so that his wet clothes could dry without getting singed.

When he was dressed, and he had made sure the letter had not gotten so wet the ink had run, Arwyn stepped out into the hallway, where Mrs Bosworth was waiting for him.

"What happened to make you leave your umbrella and sense behind in weather like this? You could have caught your death of cold out there," Mrs Bosworth chided, "First Lee and Stanley decide to play out in the rain and get sent to bed for supper, and now you."

"I received a letter," Arwyn shrugged.

"I see, and this letter contained bad news?" Mrs Bosworth asked breezily.

"It did," Arwyn confirmed with a grim expression on his face.

"I suppose this bad news needs to be shared with Lady Sarah, Mr Evans and Doctor Hales," Mrs Bosworth sighed with a sinking feeling in her chest.

"It does," the constable said.

"Then I shall prepare the household for the worst. There will be very little Christmas cheer for us I fear," Mrs Bosworth sighed and kept moving through the corridors of the house until they reached the door of the library.

"Perhaps you should come in and hear what I have to say," Arwyn said as Mrs Bosworth made to leave the constable.

"I would rather not. This year has seen so much loss, so many changes, and I do not think I can take anymore of it," Mrs Bosworth said sadly.

"I understand," the constable replied, and let the housekeeper leave before he opened the door to the library.

The room was bright and warm. There were garlands of fir hanging around the room and the scent of pine in the air was a welcome change to the wet of the outdoors. Derwyn, Miss DeVille, Lady Sarah, Doctor Hales, and his sons were all mingling around the room, enjoying drinks before dinner was served. As the door opened, Doctor Hales was the first to look up.

"Constable Evans, where have you been?" Doctor Hales asked in a jovial greeting, holding out his hand to the constable.

"A lot has happened in the last two days, I am sorry to have been detained by it," Arwyn shrugged.

Derwyn walked over to the drinks table, and poured his brother a large glass of whisky. Without saying a word, he crossed the room and pressed the glass into his brother's hand.

"What has happened?" Lady Sarah with a frown on her face.

"The body of a man was found by the reverend in the graveyard. He had been murdered. His name was S

Kvietkus," Arwyn began to explain.

"How odd, there's a man who works for a father by that name," Derwyn laughed.

"It is not odd," Arwyn said and held out the letter for his brother to read. Derwyn took the letter as Arwyn made his way to the closest sofa and sat down, nursing the glass of whisky.

"I see," Derwyn said grimly as he finished reading the letter. He walked across to Lady Sarah and gave her the letter.

As the lady began reading, the door to the library opened and Sylvia entered.

"Good evening, sorry I am late," she said cordially, warily eying the sons of the doctor.

"Miss Sylvia, can I offer you a drink?" the doctor asked.

"That would be lovely," Sylvia smiled. She could tell something was not right when she had opened the door to the library, but she did not feel comfortable enough in the grand house to ask what was going on. She walked over to join the doctor by the drinks.

"Do not worry," Doctor Hales whispered as he

handed her a gin and tonic.

Lady Sarah sighed and slowly put the letter down beside her.

"Who is investigating the murder?" Lady Sarah asked with perfect composure, though the slight shaking in her hands betrayed her emotions.

"I am, at least here in Stickleback Hollow," Arwyn replied.

"Very well," Lady Sarah said and lapsed into silent thought.

Doctor Hales moved to pick up the letter from beside her ladyship and read his old friend's words.

"Is someone going to tell the rest of us what exactly the letter says? It seems to have upset you all," Richard Hales said with a sharp edge to his voice.

"The man who was found murdered in the graveyard, he worked for my father. He was sent to us to bring news of Millie and Grace," Arwyn replied flatly.

"What news?" Gordon Hales snapped and tried to snatch the letter out of his father's hands.

"We don't know. All we know is that he was to bring news," Jack Hales told his son sternly and handed the letter to him so that he could see for himself.

"Well, someone must find out," Gordon half-shouted as he read through the letter quickly.

"Someone shall find out, but not until after dinner. You may want instant action, but all things must come in their time. Right now, it is time to eat, and then we shall deal with the mystery of Mr Kvietkus," Lady Sarah said firmly and leveled a heavy stare in Gordon's direction.

Sylvia stood by the drinks in the library and felt as though she was looking in on something very painful and private.

"I will go and see if Cooky is ready to serve," Sylvia offered and took the opportunity to leave the strangely oppressive atmosphere of the library.

What have I gotten myself into? Sylvia thought to herself as she made it out to the hall, and made her way to the kitchen, only to find that the grapevine of gossip at Grangeback had already informed all of the kitchen staff or every word that had been spoken in the library.

Chapter 11

Dinner passed in a whirl of conversation that mostly went over the head of Sylvia. She did not want to become too deeply involved as it was clear to her that she would not be needed when Grace and Millie were brought home.

She did not ask any questions or engage in any of the discussion about what action would be taken. When dinner was over, she said goodnight and retired to her bedroom.

She had been employed to help with Christmas preparations, and there were piles of gifts that needed to be wrapped, so she had no need to be involved with any of the intrigue that seemed to be absorbing the rest of the household.

Gordon Hales was adamant that he would travel to Wales in the morning and speak to Edryd directly about what he had discovered about Grace and Millie's whereabouts.

After much heated discussion, it had been his father's stern words that had convinced Gordon that it would be best not to travel alone, and instead wait until they knew more about what had happened to Mr S Kvietkus.

The S was all he was known by on the farm, according to Derwyn, as his name was Stanouslek, a Slavic name and therefore, completely unpronounceable for most of the farmhands. So for the sake of ease, he had quickly become known as S instead.

It was agreed that Sylvia would remain at the house and make the last of the preparations for Christmas with the help of Miss DeVille, Derwyn, and all three of the Hales men. Mrs Bosworth would oversee their work and the last of the shopping that had to be done.

Constable Evans would take Lady Sarah to the graveyard so that she could see the crime scene before the pair travelled to Chester to see what the police investigation in the city had uncovered.

Arwyn had explained the connection to the Russian diplomats and that there would be political complications, but Lady Sarah had no intention of being deterred. She would not mention why she was interested in the investigation, only that she intended to help the constable with her connections and influence so that the case could be closed before Christmas Day.

Doctor Hales sent Arwyn home in his coach and instructed the coachman to return to the police house in the morning to collect the constable.

Lady Sarah was the last to retire that night. She spent the hours after dinner locked in the brigadier's study, writing in depth lists that detailed everything that still needed to be done so that Mrs Bosworth could be sure that nothing was missed whilst the young lady was absent from the house.

Not only was she the last to bed, but the first to rise, even before the scullery maids. She checked over what she had written the night before and drew out a plan for the tables. There was no detail that was overlooked in her notes so by the time Mrs Bosworth entered the ballroom in search of her, Lady Sarah was satisfied that nothing would be forgotten.

"Good morning, your ladyship. Your bath is waiting for you," Mrs Bosworth said gently.

"Thank you, Mrs Bosworth. Though I doubt you will need it, here is everything that is still to be done before Christmas Day," Lady Sarah replied and handed the papers over to Mrs Bosworth.

"It is always good to have a list to work from," Mrs Bosworth replied with a smile as she looked through the papers and Lady Sarah went to wash and dress before breakfast.

Arwyn arrived not long after Lady Sarah had sat down at the breakfast table, and joined the rest of the household to eat. Richard and Gordon Hales had both spent the night in guest rooms, and both of the Baker boys had reappeared after their night of eating supper in their room.

But they were not the only guests at Grangeback that morning. Just as breakfast was being cleared away, Bosworth appeared in the dining room.

"Your ladyship, Mr Oliver Henry Brown is waiting for you in the drawing room," Bosworth announced.

"He is?" Lady Sarah replied with mild surprise.

"Yes, my lady. Do you want me to tell him that you are indisposed?" Bosworth asked.

"No, Constable Evans and I will meet with him," Lady Sarah replied, excusing herself from the breakfast table, Arwyn only a step behind her.

"She's growing into it well," Doctor Hales chuckled as the door to the dining room shut behind the departing pair.

"What?" Derwyn asked with a slight frown.

"Being lady of this house. You'd never know that she wasn't born and raised within these walls, well, if you ignore her wardrobe choices," the doctor replied.

There was no doubt that Lady Sarah belonged at Grangeback in the minds of those around her, but she still felt like a visitor. When she had been pregnant and engaged, she had begun to feel as though she was part of the fabric of life on the estate, but that had been ripped apart.

She did not know whether she would stay at the manor when the brigadier returned, but for the moment the management of the estate rested on her shoulders.

Not only did the responsibility of the estate lie with her, but she also felt that it was her duty to find Grace and Millie before she made any decision about her future.

The appearance of Mr Oliver Henry Brown had made it apparent to the young lady that there was a wide world outside of England and India that she could explore, and that it would not be the worst thing in the world to have a young and attractive American to explore the wild lands across the Atlantic with.

She did not plan to play with the young man's heart, nor did she have any intention of falling in love again, not whilst her heart ached for the man that had abandoned her.

But to have a friend to show her a new country was certainly easier than braving it alone. It was also one of the reasons that she had asked Sylvia to think about acting as her companion. Grace was a girl that would not want to leave the world she knew in England, but there was very little to keep Sylvia in England, and if she proved a good fit, Lady Sarah imagined that she would be an excellent travelling companion.

"Good morning, Mr Brown. I am afraid that you have chosen a poor morning to call upon us. The constable and I have business to attend to," Lady Sarah greeted Oliver as she entered the drawing room.

"The constable? What has happened?" Mr Brown asked with a slight frown.

"A dead body, a murder connected to the kidnapping of my lady's maid and a local charwoman, nothing out of the ordinary," Lady Sarah said teasingly.

"Then it would be a shame to miss such adventures that are so common place in England. Would you permit me to join you in your investigations?" Mr Brown asked with a wry smile.

"Constable Evans, do you have any objections?" the young lady asked, turning to Arwyn, who hovered in the doorway.

"None, my lady," Arwyn shrugged.

"Then we would be delighted to have you accompany us," Lady Sarah smiled warmly.

"Very well, lead on!" Oliver exclaimed with excitement, and Constable Evans led the way out into the cold winter morning.

The trio made their way through the snow to the graveyard beside the church. There was nothing much that could be seen thanks to the blanket of snow that covered the ground, even the footprints that the police men had left the day before had all been filled in.

After Arwyn had shown the young lady the scene and allowed her to ask questions about the body and the little that the constable had discovered.

"There's nothing else we can learn here," Lady Sarah sighed.

"So where does this trail of intrigue lead to, if there is

nothing to find here?" Oliver asked with a boyish grin.

"It leads to Chester. We'll call on the constables there and find out if they can tell us where he was staying in the city. There aren't that many inns, but it would be much quicker if we could find out which one he was staying at," Lady Sarah replied.

"Constable Cantello should know. He's not working today, but he shouldn't be too hard to find," Arwyn smiled knowingly.

The trio walked briskly back to Grangeback and took the brigadier's carriage to the city. Lady Sarah had been sure to ask Mrs Bosworth and Cooky if there was anything else they needed from the city since the investigation now led there. It took over an hour before they were ready to leave, so by the time they reached the city, it was almost midday.

"Where will we find Constable Cantello?" Mr Brown asked as the carriage slowly trundled along the city streets.

"He is normally found at the Mitre Inn on his free days," Arwyn replied.

"It will be something of a new experience for you, Mr Brown," Lady Sarah smiled.

"How so?" Oliver asked with a slight frown.

"Though I am sure that the Wild West of America holds many dangers, there are certain places in cities where you will find hives of villainy and the Mitre Inn has been one of those places. Though, it does beg the question, why is Constable Cantello there?" Lady Sarah said, directing her question at Arwyn.

"He knows the new landlord. They were boys together," Constable Evans replied.

The carriage eventually stopped outside the Mitre Inn with a lurch, and three passengers disembarked.

To Lady Sarah it felt odd to be visiting this inn without Mr Hunter at her side, but as he had elected to leave, she knew that it would not be the last time she experienced that feeling, so she did her best to push it aside.

The carriage did not wait in the street, but pulled off, heading for one of the larger and more reputable inns of the city where the carriage driver could rest the horses and find himself something to eat. Lady Sarah set a time and location for the carriage driver to meet them later before he drove on.

Arwyn held the door of the inn open for Lady Sarah to enter and allowed Mr Brown to go ahead of him.

"I am impressed," Oliver whispered to Lady Sarah.

"Oh?" she replied with interest.

"Thomas and Edward have told me all sorts of tales of your exploits since you arrived from India. I thought they had to be exaggerated, but here you are, in a place like this. I am beginning to wonder if those stories did you a disservice," Mr Brown replied out of the corner of his mouth.

"There, he's at the end of the bar," Arwyn nodded his head in the general direction of Constable Cantello, interrupting the hushed conversation. The three made their way cautiously through the inn, keeping a careful eye on those who watched them with great interest over the top of their half-empty glasses. Constable Cantello looked up as the three approached him.

"Your ladyship, this isn't the best place for you to be," he began and made to take the group outside.

"There is no time for that. We are here to ask one question, and then we will be on our way," Lady Sarah said with authority.

"Very well, what is the question?" Constable Cantello replied.

"Where was Mr Kvietkus staying here in Chester?" the young lady asked.

"Here," Constable Cantello replied with a flicker of confusion on his face.

"Then we need to look at his room," Lady Sarah said firmly.

"How do you know about Mr Kvietkus?" Constable Cantello hissed.

"I received a letter from my father. He sent Kvietkus to us by way of Chester. He was carrying information about the whereabouts of Grace and Millie," Arwyn explained.

"Always making things difficult," Constable Cantello sighed under his breath.

"Excuse me?" Lady Sarah frowned.

"Forgive me, my lady, it's just something we've taken to saying at the police headquarters," Constable Cantello blushed.

"That I am always making things difficult?" Lady Sarah asked, clearly affronted.

"Yes, my lady. It's not meant to be offensive or malicious. Only, the moment a case involves you, it is not one that will be easy to solve and most of the time, it will have a very unsatisfactory ending for my superiors' liking," Constable Cantello babbled.

"Well then, perhaps your superiors needed to change their definition of unsatisfactory then," Lady Sarah said, holding her head high in the air.

"I'll get the key," Constable Cantello said with defeat.

"It's not fair to tease us lowly peelers like that, my lady," Arwyn said with a small amount of amusement in his voice.

"Perhaps not, but he may think twice about making such a comment about me in future," Lady Sarah grinned.

It didn't take long for Constable Cantello to return with the key and he led the way up to the guest rooms without a word.

As they approached the door of Mr S Kvietkus' room, it was evident to all four of the group that they key was not necessary.

The door had been forced open. The frame of the door was splintered and parts of the lock lay in pieces on the floor.

"Always making things difficult," Arwyn said, shaking his head, causing Lady Sarah to cast a dark look in his direction.

"Stay back," Constable Cantello instructed Lady Sarah who tutted and stepped past both of the policemen to push open the door.

The room beyond was in complete disarray. There was not an item of clothing that hadn't been ripped and thrown about the place. Papers were scattered in every direction, and none of the furniture was the right way up.

"Well then, what do we do now?" Lady Sarah asked.

Chapter 12

The trip back from Chester was a sullen one. Their excursion had been for nought, and the investigation was stalled. Gordon Hales had threatened to leave for Wales that very night, and it took every amount of persuasion that his brother and father could bring to bear to keep him in the village.

Constable Evans continued to search for any clues that he could find, but his search proved to be as fruitless as the trip to Chester had been.

There was nothing to be done, and that they had come so close to discovering where Grace and Millie might be had left all in Grangeback feeling somewhat morose.

To try and take their minds off the disappointment, all energy was put towards the preparations for Christmas. Lady Sarah took charge of the decorating and oversaw the transformation of the ballroom.

Sylvia, who was not burdened with dissatisfaction, as the rest of the household was, made significant progress in the wrapping of all the gifts.

By Christmas Eve, there was nothing left to be done, except for the cooking of the great feast the following day. As Lady Sarah, Sylvia, Derwyn, and the doctor were all bound for Tatton Park, once the staff and Baker boys had eaten their evening meal, Cooky was able to begin preparations in earnest for the next day, even allowing herself an early night.

Bosworth and Mrs Bosworth elected to wait up until the household returned from the ball, and Pattinson, who had been excluded from all the Christmas excursions, was glad to have the company. The Baker boys had taken the dog under their wing for the most part, but in such a busy household, there was often so much activity that the excitable dog was overwhelmed by it all. A quiet evening by the fire whilst the Baker boys attempted to read to Mrs Bosworth was the best Christmas present Pattinson could have asked for.

Lady Sarah was dressed in her finest dress for the occasion, one she rarely wore due to the discomfort she felt in it. The crimson fabric felt appropriate for the season, the large skirt ballooned out on all sides, making it much warmer than any of her Indian inspired clothing. The corseted top was pulled tight and left her shoulders exposed. Her hair was piled on her head and had diamond pins scattered throughout it so that every time she moved her head it would catch the light at different angles.

Her neck and ears were adorned with the diamonds that had once belonged to the brigadier's wife, and her hands were covered with long silk gloves.

Mrs Bosworth had advised the young lady to wear one of her long fur cloaks to keep out the winter chill, especially with so much of Lady Sarah's shoulders showing.

Sylvia was not so grandly attired, but she looked surprisingly elegant as she descended the stairs in the entrance hall. Her hair was pinned but had mistletoe sprigs artfully placed in it.

Her dress was a deep green colour with a smaller skirt but the same off-shoulder design as Lady Sarah's dress. A simple gold chain was around her neck and a winter cloak was placed over it all. She wore lace gloves that finished at her wrist, and couldn't believe that only a few days before, she had been living on the streets of Chester.

She did not believe the change in fortunes would last long, but she was determined to enjoy it for as long as she could.

Miss DeVille wore a dress that was almost identical to

Sylvia's, save that the fabric was purple rather than green. Doctor Jack Hales, Richard, Gordon and Derwyn were all dress in black suits with white shirts, and the doctor carried a long cane. With their top hats on, the party looked perfectly suited to attend a ball.

Doctor Hales took it upon himself to be Lady Sarah's escort, whilst Richard took Sylvia's arm. Derwyn, had the arm of his fiancé, leaving Gordon to silently stew over Millie's absence.

There were so many of them bound for the ball, that both Doctor Hales and the brigadier's carriages were pressed into service. The doctor, Lady Sarah, Richard and Sylvia in the brigadier's, and Gordon, Derwyn and Miss DeVille in the doctor's.

The party was merry as they departed. Christmas was a time of year that allowed for all negativity to be swept aside and the joy of friends and family to be embraced. It was not something that was easy to do for some, but with a little practice, even Gordon had found good to hold onto this Christmas.

The drive that led up to the house at Tatton Park was littered with carriages; the drivers stood in groups, talking to one another.

"We seem to be the last to arrive," the doctor observed as he looked out of the carriage window.

"I am sure we are here in plenty of time for the party," Lady Sarah replied with a wry smile.

The driver stopped the coach and sprang from his perch to open the door for those inside. The doctor emerged first, in order to help Lady Sarah alight, followed by Richard who aided Sylvia.

"Keep hold of my arm tonight, wouldn't want you to get swept off by one of the nosy society ladies," Richard whispered to her with a smile. Sylvia responded by taking his offered arm and holding it tightly.

When Gordon, Derwyn and Miss DeVille had disembarked, the group made their way inside to be greeted by a sight that looked bot all that dissimilar from the decorations that adorned Grangeback.

Music poured out of the ballroom and dining room. The Egerton family had spared no expense on the party and each room had its own group of musicians to entertain the guests.

"Lady Sarah, Doctor Hales, thank you so much for

joining us this evening," Mrs Egerton greeted her guests from across the room as she extracted herself from a rather dull conversation with a man in a slightly worn looking suit.

"Elizabeth, how lovely to see you again," Doctor Hales bowed to the lady of the house as he spoke.

"Merry Christmas, Elizabeth, thank you for inviting us," Lady Sarah replied as she held out her hands to Mrs Egerton. The older woman took them and held them for a moment, as a sign of friendship, "May I introduce Miss Sylvia Parks, my companion, Mr Derwyn Evans and Miss Clara DeVille," Lady Sarah said introducing each in turn to Mrs Egerton.

"Wonderful to have you here to celebrate the festive season," Elizabeth Egerton smiled and nodded to each in turn.

"Of course you remember my sons," the doctor said.

"Ah yes, Richard, Gordon, you must tell us all about University. But first, we must find you something to drink. My husband is talking with his colleagues in the library, I don't advise being dragged into their musings about the world - very depressing. I would also avoid getting roped into conversation with Mr Nash, he is a kind man, but rather dull and has no real influence anymore," Elizabeth said, nodding in the direction of the gentleman she had been speaking with when they had arrived. "Come, this way."

"You have such elegant decorations, and the music is sublime," Lady Sarah said as Elizabeth Egerton steered the party through the throng to the ballroom.

"Thank you, my dear, I am looking forward to seeing how you have prepared Grangeback for the feast tomorrow. The first year always feels like such a test, but it does mean that the second year is much easier. When you have hosted as many parties and balls as we have, it becomes almost second nature," Elizabeth replied.

"You will have to offer me advice on any improvements I can make for next year," Lady Sarah smiled graciously.

"It would be my pleasure. Ah! Wilbraham, darling boy, come here," Elizabeth suddenly called out and waved for her son to approach.

"You called, mother? Ah, Lady Sarah, Richard, Gordon, doctor, how wonderful to see you all," Wilbraham said with a grin as he joined the group.

"Would you be so good as to find some refreshments

for our guests, you can make your own introductions, I am sure. If you will excuse me, the duties of the hostess are never-ending," Elizabeth said and quickly made her way across the room to where the housekeeper was looking agitated.

"I don't think she has ever really enjoyed a ball here in her life," Wilbraham mused as he watched his mother depart.

"What a wonderful surprise to see you looking so well," Lady Sarah said, drawing Wilbraham's attention back to her.

"Indeed, I have been back in England for a few weeks, but I have been touring the northern country with a friend. I left him to come back for Christmas, I'm not sure my mother would forgive if I was not here for this," Wilbraham replied and led the way over to where a footman was serving wassail.

"Well, I am glad, it has been too long," Lady Sarah said with genuine joy in her voice.

"Then I hope you will do me the honour of waltzing with me," Wilbraham said with a bow.

"If the doctor doesn't mind," Lady Sarah said with a

wry smile in Jack Hales' direction.

"I shall save m dancing until later this evening, look after her," the doctor said with a warning edge to his voice. His eyes locked with Wilbraham's, and for a moment the two men shared a silent conversation. A form of understanding seemed to pass between them, and before Lady Sarah knew it, the doctor had taken her punch glass so that Wilbraham could lead her to the dance floor.

"There are some people here tonight that wish to meet you," Wilbraham said as the two moved effortlessly across the dance floor.

"Oh?" Lady Sarah asked with surprise.

"Yes, my youngest brother and sister, Charles and Charlotte," Wilbraham replied.

"Oh, how wonderful, I did not think that I would ever make their acquaintance. Your mother keeps them quite well hidden," Lady Sarah mused with a playful glint in her eye.

"I am not sure she could keep you away from them after all the stories they have been told. My dear cousin, Oliver, has not been helping in that regard. He seems to be quite taken with you," Wilbraham said with amusement.

"Is that so?" Lady Sarah tried to sound disinterested,

but could not help but blush.

"Do not fear, tonight I plan to monopolise all of your time, aside from allowing you to meet my brother and sister," Wilbraham replied.

"Who else do I know that s here tonight?' Lady Sarah asked as she tried to scan those who were dancing alongside them.

"Miss Beaumont and Mr Claydon are here. The explorer always knows how to entertain the more inquisitive of my mother's guests," Wilbraham laughed.

"Ah, so they are in the sitting room, I suppose?" Lady Sarah asked.

"They are indeed. My brothers are all here, but there is one other person here that you may have heard of, even though I doubt you know them personally," Wilbraham said as he tried to think through the guest list.

"Who is that?" Lady Sarah asked.

"The Russian Ambassador, Carlo Pozzo di Borgo . A Corsican who fought against Napoleon at Waterloo, but his title should tell you much about the man," Wilbraham said as the waltz finished and new music rose up to replace it.

"Is he indeed, how interesting," Lady Sarah replied,

her eyes narrowing slightly as she spoke.

"But let us talk of joyful things, not dull politics. What delights can we expect to find at Grangeback tomorrow?" Wilbraham asked with a devilish glint in his eye.

"Now, Mr Egerton, you should know that a lady does not reveal such things! What surprises would there be if I told you all now?" Lady Sarah said with a grin, the Russian Ambassador pushed aside in her mind, but not completely forgotten.

The pair danced for over half an hour before Wilbraham led her from the floor.

"I thought we would dance all night," Lady Sarah commented with a slight edge of disappointment to her voice.

"My lady, we will return to it shortly, but I thought we should take the opportunity to meet with some guests that crave an audience with you," Wilbraham replied with a smile.

"And who are these guests?" Lady Sarah asked with suspicion.

"Lady Sarah, may I introduce Miss Charlotte and Mr Charles Egerton, the youngest of my darling siblings, and twins that could rival your infamous Baker boys for hi-jinx," Wilbraham said as he stopped before a young boy and girl who looked rather out of place amongst all the finely dressed adults.

"What a pleasure to meet you both!" Lady Sarah beamed with genuine delight as she shook each of their hands.

"Thomas and Edward told us stories about you. Are they true?" Charlotte asked bluntly.

"Charlotte!" Wilbraham scolded her.

"Of course, you don't think that your brothers would lie to you, do you?" Lady Sarah replied as she looked Charlotte square in the eye.

"No. But father says there is a first time for everything, " Charlotte shrugged.

"And he would be correct," a booming voice called from behind Lady Sarah. She turned to see the familiar faces of Mr Claydon and Miss Beaumont stood there, "But I do not think your brothers have lied to you, young miss. Her ladyship has the heart of an adventurer and the spirit of the wildest tiger from the jungles of India. Do not doubt that every story they have told you is true. I am all but certain that they will have toned down the stores to make them seem more realistic!" Mr Claydon laughed.

"Wilbraham, do you know Mr Claydon and Miss Beaumont?" Lady Sarah asked, trying to divert the attention of the gawping children to the old explorer and his companion.

"I have never had the pleasure, but the legend of such a great explorer always goes before him," Wilbraham beamed and offered his hand in friendship to Mitchell Claydon.

"And the respect of man that has fought and served around the world is always welcome," Mr Claydon replied.

Miss Beaumont curtseyed to Captain Egerton, but as she preferred to remain in Mr Claydon's shadow, did not address Wilbraham directly.

The two men began discussing their experiences in the many different countries they had seen, allowing Miss Beaumont to come to Lady Sarah's side.

"It is lovely to see you looking so well," Miss Beaumont said softly.

"Thank you. I am looking forward to hosting you tomorrow, as well as these two rapscallions," Lady Sarah said, flashing a smile in the direction of the twins.

"I see, and what would these rapscallions be better known as?" Miss Beaumont asked, casting the trained eye of a governess over the two Egerton children.

"Charles and Charlotte Egerton," Lady Sarah introduced the pair.

"Ah! I know of their exploits already. Their former governess is a friend of mine," Miss Beaumont replied, looking at the two children with suspicion.

"We promised we would be good tonight. Mother said we couldn't come if we weren't good," Charlotte pouted.

"Well then, I expect she will say the same thing to you tomorrow. But I don't doubt that you will be drawn into some form of mischief by the Baker boys," Lady Sarah did her best to suppress a giggle at the thought of the four children forming an unholy alliance to cause as much trouble as possible for Mrs Bosworth and Cooky.

"We won't be naughty, we promise," Charles replied.

"No, we want to meet your dog," Charlotte blurted out.

"Ah, now I understand why you have promised to be good! You were bribed with the promise of Pattinson!" Lady

Sarah said with a grin.

"No!" the twins chorused, causing Miss Beaumont to laugh.

"Peace, young ones. Go enjoy the party. There are treats galore on the table in the hallway that no one has touched," Miss Beaumont said gently and the youngest Egerton children sprang into a run to seize the Christmas delights before anyone else did.

"They are sweet children, though they are my cousins, so perhaps I have to think that," Mr Oliver Henry Brown said as he sauntered over to where Lady Sarah and Miss Beaumont were standing.

"Perhaps, but I find them to dear hearts and they are certainly no relation of mine," Lady Sarah replied, showing no surprise at the gentleman's sudden appearance, "Mr Brown, have you met Miss Beaumont?"

"No, but it is my great pleasure to make the acquaintance of any that call such an elegant lady their friend," Mr Brown drawled as he took Miss Beaumont by the hand and kissed it. Lady Sarah and Miss Beaumont both blushed.

"Mr Brown, the gossips of Stickleback Hollow say that

you have recently arrived from America. Do you plan to stay long?" Miss Beaumont asked as she gracefully withdrew her hand from Oliver's grasp and tried to ignore the flush in her cheeks.

"I plan to stay as long as the country is amenable to my presence," Mr Brown replied, casting a long look in Lady Sarah's direction as he spoke.

"Ah! This must be the American I have heard so much about," Mr Claydon boomed, as he and Wilbraham rejoined the ladies.

"Mr Mitchell Claydon, this is my cousin, Mr Oliver Henry Brown," Wilbraham introduced the explorer as he looked between the American and Lady Sarah.

"Good to meet you, pleasure, pleasure," Mr Claydon said as he shook Mr Brown's hand with enthusiasm, "You must tell me all about your country, is it as wild as they say? What about the natives? Come, come, we must find you a drink to loosen that tongue of yours and you can regale me and my dear Miss Beaumont with your stories," Mitchell said as he took Oliver by the elbow and marched him off in search of Wassail.

"Enjoy the rest of the party. I am sure I will see you

later," Miss Beaumont said with an amused smile as she took her leave of Lady Sarah and followed after Mr Claydon and Mr Brown.

"Will you honour me with another waltz? Miss Sylvia seems to have charmed Richard into never leaving the floor," Wilbraham chuckled, "Then I promise that I shall return you to the doctor."

"Of course. Sylvia is a woman of many talents and charms, I am surprised she has only caused Richard to become infatuated," Lady Sarah replied as she took Wilbraham's hand and allowed him to lead her to the dance floor.

"Well, my cousin is certainly infatuated with you, my lady," Wilbraham said flatly.

"Is that a note of jealousy?" Lady Sarah asked with a wry smile on her face.

"You should not jest about such things. Besides, I was under the impression that your heart belonged to another," Wilbraham said in an off-hand manner.

Lady Sarah's jaw tightened slightly and she looked away from Wilbraham.

"I'm sorry. It was not very gentlemanly of me to bring

up such a thing, but for what it is worth, I would not be quick to try and find another to fill the void in your heart. It is always a mistake," Wilbraham said in a low voice.

"I appreciate your concern, but I would rather not discuss Mr Hunter, or his departure," Lady Sarah replied in a flat tone.

"Very well, then perhaps you would accept advice of a different nature?" Wilbraham asked as he pulled Lady Sarah closer to him so that he could whisper in her ear.

"Wilbraham, what on earth are you doing?" Lady Sarah protested but found that she couldn't escape Wilbraham's strong arms.

"You are in greater danger than you know," Wilbraham whispered.

"What?" the young lady asked, her eyes wide with alarm.

"Carlo is an honourable man, but not a man to be crossed. There are those within his embassy that are merciless with political ambitions that drive them to despicable deeds. Whatever has caused you to become known to the ambassador, I do not know, but I know that if you get in his way, he will harm you. Please, be as careful in your dealings with him as you are when you place your feet when dance," Wilbraham continued. The moment he was finished, he released Lady Sarah. The two continued to dance until the orchestra had finished, Lady Sarah's mind whirling.

When the dance was over, Wilbraham delivered the young lady back into the company of Doctor Hales.

"Have you enjoyed yourself this evening?" the doctor asked cheerfully, his cheeks slightly reddened by the Wassail.

"It has been an enlightening evening," Lady Sarah replied.

"What is wrong?" the doctor frowned.

"I do not yet know, but I intend to find out," Lady Sarah replied.

Chapter 13

Captain Wilbraham Egerton took his leave of the Grangeback party. Nothing would have pleased him more than to spend the whole of the ball in their company, but he had a niggling doubt that he could not wrestle into silence.

Though he had warned Lady Sarah to be careful, he could not shake the feeling that she was in immediate danger. The only way he could think of to stop these feelings was to speak to his brother about the situation. William Egerton had been engaged in political conversations since the ball began and he would not be difficult to find.

"Wilbraham, there you are! Where have you been hiding?" Thomas Egerton called out to his older brother as he spotted him in the hallway.

"Oh Thomas, Edward, why are you not dancing with your companions?" Wilbraham replied as he looked up to see his brothers approaching.

"They are being captive by mother. She insists she needs them to help her oversee the party. Now come, older brother, tell us where have you been!" Edward said enthusiastically.

"Waltzing with Lady Sarah to keep her out of our cousin's grasp," Wilbraham said dryly.

"Oh ho! I told you! Hunter leaves and our dear brother throws his hat at her ladyship," Thomas crowed.

"That is not it at all. I admire her ladyship, but that is all. Now lower your voice," Wilbraham warned his brothers.

"You are wound too tightly, brother. Thomas was merely jesting. Is there something wrong?" Edward asked.

"No, but I am looking for Carlo Pozzo di Borgo, have you seen him?" Wilbraham asked as he glanced about.

"Yes, he was talking to William, but he was called away. He went outside not two minutes ago," Thomas replied.

"Thank you. Oh, could you both go to the ballroom and ensure that Lady Sarah and the party from Grangeback don't leave just yet?" Wilbraham asked as he began to move towards the door.

"Why?" Edward frowned.

"Because I said so," Wilbraham replied. Thomas looked at Edward and shrugged. The two shaking their heads, set off for the ballroom to do as their brother asked.

"Someone should tell him that we aren't in the army," Edward muttered under his breath.

Wilbraham made his way through the milling throng of party guests to the grand entrance to the great house. He paused in the doorway to drink in the cold night air and reached into his inside pocket in search of a cigar.

Putting it to his lips, he took a moment to casually glance about until he saw the Russian ambassador moving across the lawn towards the summer house.

Lighting the cigar, Wilbraham followed at a casual pace, trying to make it seem as though he was not in pursuit of the ambassador.

The Russian moved quickly, not bothering to look over his shoulder. He did not see danger lurking in shadows, he was that danger. His heavy footsteps obliterated any sound that Wilbraham's feet made.

There was a single lamp lit in the window of the summerhouse, something that struck Wilbraham as odd. Not only because everyone was supposed to be in the main house enjoying the festivities, but also because his mother was always worried about soot on the glass panes and never allowed any lamps to be lit and placed in any of the windows.

A thin shadow stood in the darkness behind the lamp. Wilbraham could barely make out the figure as he strained to see, but it was clear to him that the Russian Ambassador was going to meet with whoever waited in the dark.

The glass of the summerhouse was not thick and the wooden frame meant that it did little to muffle sound, both from within and without.

Wilbraham was also painfully aware that whoever had set the lamp would be looking out for the ambassador and unlikely to take kindly to him being followed. He edged around the side of the house, heading towards the stables, making sure he was hidden in the umbra of the house and trees as he stalked as silently as he could up to the side of the summer house.

As he approached, he could hear the sound of arguing coming from within.

"What could be so important that you need to drag me out from a Christmas party to talk to you?" Ambassador Carlo Andrea asked in irritation. He spoke in heavily accented Russian, but, thanks to his schooling, Wilbraham had no problem understanding him.

"I am sorry, my lord, but it is important. The traitor Kvietkus, there is a woman whom he was supposed to see. We suspect that she is plotting something terrible. She must be removed as quickly as possible," the shadow replied. His accent was flawless but familiar to Wilbraham.

"A woman? Don't be so foolish," the ambassador said dismissively.

"Do you forget about Fitzwilliam and John Smith? These women that rise to such places are dangerous. They can bring down nations. I will not see the Czar brought to shame by any woman," the shadow said with venom.

"And what can a woman in this land do to the Czar? There are far greater threats to his life that you should be concerned with," Carlo Andrea spat back.

"She is a woman that both Fitzwilliam and John Smith fear. You would be wise to treat her as an enemy as well," the shadow replied.

"I will do nothing without evidence. I am still waiting for you to bring Kvietkus to me so that the allegations against him can be either proven or cast aside as nonsense. Until I have seen the man, I will not fear a woman. I expect you will bring Kvietkus to me soon, so until you are ready to do so, I have engagements to attend," the ambassador said as he turned on his heel and marched out of the summerhouse.

"And I will do what I must to keep my country safe from all enemies," the shadow said under his breath, but it was not quiet enough to escape the listening ears of Captain Wilbraham.

He did not know who the shadow was, but he did know that the only woman he could have been talking about was Lady Sarah.

He sat, surrounded by the darkness, as the light in the summer house was put out and the mysterious figure departed. Wilbraham did not want to move until he was sure that the man was gone. He listened intently for the sound of gravel crunching underfoot as the man walked into the night.

When Wilbraham was certain that the man had gone far enough that he would not see the captain, Wilbraham stood up slowly and made his way back to the party.

"Wilbraham, what were you doing outside?" the surprised voice of the Russian ambassador asked as he noticed Wilbraham entering the hall.

"I went to check on the horses. I wanted to make sure that they had been properly taken care of. In all the excitement of the party, I thought they might have been forgotten," Wilbraham lied with a smile.

"Ah, I trust the stable hands were diligent in their duty?" Carlo-Andrea asked.

"They were, my fears were groundless, but the time I do not check, will be the time that they are forgotten," Wilbraham replied warmly.

"Of course, of course, I must return to the discussions in the library, but Merry Christmas, my friend," the ambassador said, shaking Wilbraham's hand.

"And to you, sir," Wilbraham grinned. The ambassador moved quickly through the thinning crowd in the hallway to where the politicians were swilling brandy and smoking cigars.

"Wilbraham! There you are, what is this nonsense that your brothers tell me, why can't our friends from Grangeback leave?" Elizabeth Egerton demanded of her son.

"Because mother, I am going back with them this evening, and I did not want them to leave without me," Wilbraham replied as he turned to see his mother, flanked by Thomas' wife, Charlotte, and Edward's fiancé, Mary, on either side.

"What? Why?" Elizabeth Egerton cried.

"I made a promise to Hunter. Do not fret, mother, I will see you at the dinner table tomorrow," Wilbraham soothed his mother as took hold of her upper arms and kissed her on the forehead.

Elizabeth Egerton could say no more as her son moved quickly away from her and into the ballroom, leaving the astounded woman behind.

He had not lied to his mother. Before he had parted from Mr Hunter to return for the Christmas festivities, he had promised to protect Lady Sarah until Alex was ready to return. It was not a promise that he made lightly, nor was it a promise that he intended to break.

Though he doubted that the Russian ambassador was a threat to Lady Sarah's safety, he was utterly convinced that the man he had been talking to would have no qualms about killing the young lady and framing some poor idiot for the murder. There was little danger that evening, or on Christmas Day. There were too many people, too many eyes, too much attention for anything to be attempted, but on Boxing Day when the staff of Grangeback were all absent, and the village was settled into the dozy haze of the second day of Christmas, that was when the strike would come, and Wilbraham did not intend to allow the shadowy figure to succeed.

Chapter 14

The Reverend Percy Butterfield did not disappoint his congregation as he spoke to them from the pulpit on Christmas morning. His voice had thundered and reached up through the rafters to heaven itself.

"The lesson that we must go out with this fine Christmas morning is when it comes to facing our own giants of fear and doubt, do not despair, as nothing is impossible when the Lord God has made a way for it to come. Mary bore the son of God, the sons of Abraham went forth and multiplied to fill the earth. Throughout the Bible, there is testament after testament to this very simple lesson. Nothing is impossible with God. This is the word of the Lord," the Reverend said as he closed his sermon.

"Thanks be to God," the congregation replied.

"And on this Christmas morning, when we celebrate the coming of our Lord, Jesus Christ, there has been no better time to pass the peace amongst us. May peace be with you."

"And also with you," the congregation chorused before turning to one another to shake hands and wish peace upon their neighbours.

"May the Lord bless this day and the time we share together in breaking of bread. Go forth in his name, and Merry Christmas," the reverend finished and made his way from the pulpit to the door of the church where he spoke to each of his parishioners in turn as they departed.

"It has always seemed so odd to me," Wilbraham commented as he walked beside Lady Sarah and the doctor in the churchyard.

"What?" the doctor asked.

"That a man of such faith and conviction as Percy Butterfield should be nothing more than a simple vicar," Wilbraham replied.

"Is there a higher calling than being such? He brings comfort and light to this community, shares in all the joys and pain of the people here, what more could a man of the cloth want?" Lady Sarah frowned.

"I suppose there is not, especially if the reverend feels that God has called him to serve in his current role. It is quite different to those who are hoping to be named Archbishop," Wilbraham shrugged.

"Then perhaps it is a case of being happier as a simple

priest than unhappy not being named Archbishop," Doctor Hales winked.

"It was a terribly good sermon though," Lady Sarah said, changing the subject.

"I do not believe I have ever heard him deliver a bad one. When he wishes to discuss steam engines though, that is quite a different matter. Now come, or your guests shall all arrive before you!" Wilbraham said, clapping his hands and ushering Lady Sarah to her carriage.

Nobody had questioned Wilbraham's sudden decision to accompany the party back to Grangeback after the ball. The doctor had felt that perhaps the captain's influence would go some way to helping to heal the lady's broken heart and keep from the dangers of investigating the murder of Mr S Kvietkus.

As far as the physician was concerned, the celebration of Christmas with the village and their friends from Tatton Park was far more important than indulging Lady Sarah's habit of discovering trouble.

Jack Hales had begun to feel his age since taking up residence at Grangeback in the absence of the brigadier. The constant ebb and flow of people around the house, the bustle of life without any quiet moments alone to sit with his thoughts, and on top of that there was the constant fear that Lady Sarah would barrel headlong into danger without any warning was putting a great deal of stress on his heart.

To have a day of simple joy and celebration with his friends, family, and neighbours was something he had been looking forward to.

Sylvia had left the church as soon as the sermon was over, with Cooky, Mrs Bosworth, Bosworth and Richard Hales. There was nothing in particular that Richard needed to do to contribute to the day, but he had been glad of the excuse to escape his brother's foul mood.

Gordon Hales had been in a bad mood since he had first laid eyes on Sylvia. The depth of his anger ranged from white-hot rage to irritable, but it had never completely disappeared. Richard loved his brother, but he was not prepared to have all the joy sucked out of Christmas by his brother.

Gordon had elected to go in his father's buggy to the church, and spend some time alone with his thoughts before the celebrations of the day began.

He had been surprised at how much the presence of

Sylvia and the news that Arywn's father had information about the whereabouts of Millie and Grace had shocked him.

It had been months since there had been any word about the missing girls, and Gordon had begun to come to terms with the fact that they were most likely dead and never coming home again. But the smallest glimmer of hope had thrown everything into chaos in his mind once again.

He had sat with his father, brother, and the rest of the contingent from Grangeback during the service, and had been dragged aside by Derwyn as soon as the reverend had finished speaking to talk with him, Arwyn and Miss DeVille

The doctor knew that Derwyn and Arwyn would make sure that his son made it to the feast, so he settled back in the carriage and closed his eyes.

The driver flicked the reins and the carriage lurched away from the church carrying Lady Sarah, Wilbraham and the doctor.

Wilbraham knew that it wouldn't be long until his family arrived at Grangeback either. They did not attend the service at the church in Stickleback Hollow but had to appear at the church in Knutsford instead. However, Vicar Robert Clowes was much briefer in his teachings than the Reverend

Percy Butterfield was, so they would be arriving at Grangeback sooner than Mrs Bosworth would be expecting.

However, being at the manor to greet his family and the rest of the guests of Grangeback that day was not the primary reason that Wilbraham had wanted to leave the church.

He did not feel the lady was safe outside; especially in a milling crowd. In her own house, where all the guests were known and servants watched over everything, things were a lot more secure. Wilbraham was almost certain the Russians would not do anything to harm Lady Sarah in such a public setting, but he did not want to risk her life unnecessarily.

As the carriage lurched along the narrow road that ran from the church down to the manor house, Wilbraham prayed silently for the return of Mr Hunter.

The time the captain had spent with the groundskeeper touring the northern counties had shown Wilbraham that Alex was still in love with Lady Sarah and that it was only pain, grief, and guilt that had forced him to leave her and his home behind.

The captain only hoped that the groundskeeper would realise how much he loved Lady Sarah and return to her before his cousin could enchant the young lady away.

Wilbraham was roused from his thoughts by the carriage stopping outside of Grangeback. Once the passengers had disembarked from the carriage, the driver was quick about returning to the stables so that the grooms could see to the horses and all of them could make their way inside to the meal.

It was a hard thing to coordinate sometimes, but as the majority of people arriving for Christmas dinner would be making their way from the church on foot, only one of the grooms would need to wait to take care of the horses of the Egertons when they arrived. After their horses were taken care of, the groom would be able to join everyone else for the feast.

The dinner itself was unusual as the tables were piled high with food by the maids, footmen and Cooky, but no one was stood waiting to serve or clear the room.

Lady Sarah hurried into the house to check that everything was where it should be. Wilbraham and the doctor did not need to hurry. Cooky could be heard shouting instructions in the kitchen as metal clanked and feet thundered across the floors.

"Merry Christmas, gentlemen," Mrs Bosworth greeted the two men as they took off their cloaks in the hallway and hung them on one of the cloak racks in the men's cloakroom. Normally, Bosworth, the butler, would have been on hand to take the cloaks from the two men, but he was advising the footmen of what they needed to do before the meal.

By the time the rest of the guests arrived Bosworth and a few of his best footmen would be on hand to take the cloaks from the men as they passed through the doors of Grangeback, whereas Mrs Bosworth and some of the best maids would be waiting in the ladies' cloakroom to take the garments from the ladies and help them with any emergencies that required a feminine touch.

Hosting the Christmas Dinner was a wonderful event for the village, but extremely hard on the household staff until they sat down to eat. There was a lot that needed to be done and even more that had to be cleared away between courses. However, not one of them grumbled about the work as they all knew their reward was a day without duties and generous Christmas gifts from the brigadier.

"Merry Christmas, Mrs Bosworth, is everything prepared?" the doctor asked clapping his hands together with glee.

"Yes, doctor. The mulled wine is waiting for you in the ballroom. I am sure that you both will benefit from the warmth, chase away the chill," Mrs Bosworth said, indicating that the two men should proceed down the hallway.

"A capital idea, Mrs Bosworth, come doctor, mulled wine is a rarity in the officer's mess," Wilbraham declared with enthusiasm as he slapped the doctor on the shoulder and the pair made their way through the house.

There was no thought in either man's head that they should offer their assistance to the servants as they bustled around. Even if there had been, it would have been driven out of their heads by the sight that greeted them as they entered the ballroom.

The candles in the giant chandeliers glittered as reflections in the ornate crystal that surrounded them. Tables lay in lines and were piled with cutlery, glassware, napkins, nuts, fruit and the sweet treats that Lady Sarah had bought in Chester.

Two wide tables lay at either end of the lines, one was Lady Sarah's table, and there was space upon it for the meats to be placed so they could be carved in front of her guests.

The other table lay waiting for the rest of the food for the feast to be laid upon it.

In the corner of the room, there were chairs laid out for the orchestra that would perform. They travelled from Manchester every year to perform at Grangeback. They were paid well for their trouble, something that was especially welcomed by their families. The money that the brigadier gave them often paid to keep their children in shoe leather and the bellies of their families filled through the leaner months of the year.

To the left of the door was a table that was covered with jugs of mulled wine, mead, cider and cordials. But the most interesting feature in the room was one that seemed most odd to the two men.

In the opposite corner to the orchestra chairs, there stood a giant fir tree. It stood in a bucket of sand, though it could not be seen due to the sea of gifts that were spread out beneath and around it.

"Why a tree?" the doctor frowned as he looked at it with fascination.

"I have heard that it is a popular thing to do in Germany. Perhaps, as a relative of our new queen, Lady

Sarah erected it as a sign of respect. I doubt that it is an Indian custom," Wilbraham replied as he seized one of the jugs of mulled with and filled two of the glasses on Lady Sarah's table with the liquid.

"Whatever the reason, it will certainly be a novelty for today's guests. Lady Sarah has also outdone herself with all the gifts. I imagine that Derwyn, Sylvia and Miss DeVille all spent many sleepless nights wrapping them and putting those labels on each," the doctor sighed as he accepted one of the glasses of mulled wine from the captain.

"A novelty? My dear doctor, it will be something that they remember and talk of for years to come," Lady Sarah announced her arrival into the ballroom with good humour. She had changed from the dress she wore to church into an elegant gown of royal blue silk edged with white lace.

"There will be no forgetting today, that is for sure," Wilbraham agreed.

"My guests are arriving, so please come sit beside me for the feast, I fear that today will be something of a whirlwind and I need some steady hands beside me," Lady Sarah grinned, and the two men agreed to her request.

The village arrived as a great mass of people, with

only those travelling in carriages arriving before the main horde.

Richard, Sylvia, Derwyn, Miss DeVille and Gordon were the first of the guests to be greeted by Bosworth, Mrs Bosworth and their aides. They were followed by the Egerton family, in its entirety, and Mr Oliver Henry Brown.

Finally, the Reverend Percy Butterfield lead the villagers of Stickleback Hollow to the front doors. The relative quiet of the house was filled with noise and revelry, and it was not long before the sound of the orchestra playing Christmas carols drew all of Lady Sarah's guests to the ballroom.

It was a scene of great joy, not often seen by those from outside the village. It was the coming together of every social class, something that made the Egertons feel somewhat uncomfortable.

There was a reason that servants did not socialise with their employers, and it was unseemly for the class boundaries to be crossed on any other day of the year. But for Christmas Day, it was tolerable.

"What an altruistic spirit you have, my dear," Mrs Egerton praised Lady Sarah as she watched the villagers drinking and eating their way through the lavish feast.

"Truly a Christian attitude to exemplify during this festive season," Mr Egerton agreed.

The feast passed as quickly as Lady Sarah feared it would. Once the food was finished, the gifts were distributed to the assembled guests by Lady Sarah, with the help of Sylvia, Miss DeVille, Derwyn and Richard.

No one was overlooked, not even the members of the orchestra. There were cries of delight and gratitude, and it was hard to see how anyone could not feel blessed and happy in such an environment. Yet, Arwyn's mind was troubled, and the look on his face did not go unnoticed by Wilbraham Egerton.

Chapter 15

"Come, my friend, you need to unburden yourself," Wilbraham whispered in the constable's ear as the gift-giving turned to carolling and dancing.

Arwyn looked surprised to see the captain at his shoulder but allowed him to steer him from the ballroom to the library. The servants were clearing the tables of the empty plates and used cutlery, so paid little attention to the two men who slipped through the house.

When they were safely encased in the quiet and calm of the library, Wilbraham spoke.

"It takes a serious matter to cloud a day such as today. If you will tell me what troubles you, I will do the same," the captain said slowly as he poured them both a glass of whisky.

"I received a letter this morning. I suspect I received it yesterday, but I didn't find it until today," Arwyn began, his voice shaking.

"And what was in this letter?" Wilbraham asked

patiently.

"It was from Mr Hunter. He told me about meeting you on the road north, and the time you spent together. He also said that after you parted ways, he happened upon some information that he believes could lead him to find Grace and Millie. He is unlikely to return for quite some time," Arwyn replied and drag deeply from the glass of single malt.

"I see. Are you concerned for his safety or concerned that he may never return home again?" Wilbraham inquired.

"Both. Since the man carrying news of Grace and Millie was murdered, it has become clear that searching for them is too dangerous to be undertaken alone. Alex doesn't know the danger he is in," Arwyn shook his head and sighed.

"Of all the men I have met in my life, there is none that I would consider as brave, resourceful, and hard to kill as Mr Hunter. He will not blunder about blindly, nor take foolish risks unless a certain lady is involved. I would not worry about him as much as I would be concerned about her," Wilbraham shrugged.

"You are concerned about Lady Sarah? Why?" Arwyn asked with bemusement.

"I am concerned about her safety and her heart. For her heart's sake, I would hurry the return of Mr Hunter. My cousin has become somewhat enamoured with the legend of Lady Sarah and fancies himself in love. He is a good man, but he is not in love. I would not wish a foolish love affair upon either of them. Hunter returning home would be the best and quickest way for all three to find happiness. But there is such stupidity where love is concerned," Wilbraham laughed to himself.

"And why are you concerned for her safety?" Arwyn asked as he sat on one of the sofas and leaned forward on his knees.

"Last night, I followed the Russian ambassador as he stepped out into the gardens. He was meeting with a man who will stop at nothing to keep his secrets. Right now, Lady Sarah is a threat to him. Today, there was nothing to fear. There are too many people here that she knows and trusts, she is too well protected. But tomorrow, the house will all but empty and Lady Sarah will be in more danger than I think either of us can conceive at this moment," Wilbraham took a deep breath and exhaled slowly.

"What can we do?" Arwyn asked.

"Firstly, I would write back to Mr Hunter at the address in his letter. Tell him of everything that has happened here. Of Oliver, of the murder and the danger to Lady Sarah. Then I would suggest that we both stay here until we can be certain that she is safe," Wilbraham replied.

A scream and yelling in the hallway interrupted any further conversation and caused the two men to scramble for the door as fast as they could.

As they stumbled into the hall, they saw the source of the commotion. Two of the maids were in tears, sobbing to each other. Behind them, Cooky and Mrs Egerton had four children by the ears. Lee, Stanley, Charlotte and Charles.

"We should get back to the party, no telling what we'll miss," Wilbraham winked and marched over to his mother to find out what such an unholy alliance of mischief-makers had been doing on such a holy day.

Chapter 16

It was almost midnight when the last of the guest left Grangeback Manor. The orchestra had stayed until the bitter end and been well compensated with twice their agreed fee. Lady Sarah had paid each of them personally and thanked them for their sacrifice of the day with their families.

For many of them, Christmas Day was not as important as Boxing Day. But it was a long way home in the dark and late night. They had come in hired coaches and driven the horses themselves.

The grooms were in no fit state to help put the horses back in their traces, so Wilbraham had helped, along with the Egertons' driver.

Wilbraham also explained to his mother that he would be home on 27th December as he was going to remain to help with the clearing of the ballroom.

Elizabeth Egerton had protested, to begin with, but as her son shared her stubborn streak, she soon gave it up as a lost cause.

"In that case, your brother and sister can stay too. They should do something to apologise for their behaviour this evening," Mrs Egerton had said and left Charlotte and Charles in their brother's care.

All three had argued with their mother about the idea, but Elizabeth had climbed into the family carriage without even acknowledging a word that her children said. Edward and Thomas had climbed into the carriage wearing smug faces, doing their best not to laugh, should their mother decide that they would also be staying behind to assist the household staff.

Neither the Honourable Wilbraham Egerton nor the Honourable William Egerton paid any mind to the affairs of the family. The pair were engrossed in a conversation about the finer politics of the opium situation in China.

Mrs Bosworth had not flinched even for a moment when presented with the task of finding beds for Charles and Charlotte Egerton, though both were warned that the housekeeper was not a woman to cross twice in one day. Any plans for further chaos were thwarted for at least a few hours, though Wilbraham felt very uneasy about his brother and sister being in the house with the potential danger to

Lady Sarah looming.

By the time the ballroom was cleared and cleaned, not a soul in the house could keep their eyes open. Pattinson had been left outside during the feast, guarding the horses in the stables. He had been rewarded with leftover meat from the feast and trotted happily beside Lady Sarah to guard her whilst she slept.

Charles and Charlotte had both been allowed to play with the dog whilst the process of returning the ballroom to normal was undertaken, and they were both disappointed when Mrs Bosworth and Wilbraham sent them off to bed.

Richard and Gordon had both elected to stay the night at the house, rather than making the journey down to the village to their father's home.

Cooky had made sure that there was enough food for the household, even with the additional guests for at least three days, even though most of the staff would be back before midnight on Boxing Day.

Some of it would need heating over a fire or in the oven, but she knew that the constable was capable enough to take care of simpler cooking tasks.

Lady Sarah and the doctor made sure that the Boxing

Day gifts were all waiting for the staff outside their bedroom doors before they went to bed themselves.

By the time that Pattinson woke Lady Sarah, needing to go outside to relieve himself, the boxes had all been opened and the staff had all departed. They would enjoy their day away from the house, but they all would happily return to Grangeback once the day was over. The manor was their home, and it was one of the better places to work in the county, if not the country.

They were respected by their employers, and though exacting in their standards, Cooky, Bosworth and Mrs Bosworth were not cruel to those that worked under them. The staff rooms were better than most homes could boast, and their wages were fair for the hours that they worked.

A day or two without the servants in the house was not much of a sacrifice for the brigadier or Lady Sarah to endure to thank the staff for all they did the rest of the year.

Rather than return to her bed, Lady Sarah dressed in one of her warmer dresses that Miss Baker had created for her. The dress was unusual in that it fused the fashions of India with those of England, which also meant that there were few occasions that Lady Sarah could wear it. The many layers of thick and thin fabrics made the dress extremely warm and flattering. The pale blue silk in stark contrast to the deep purple velvet made the dress just as striking for the colours as the mixture of fabrics and styles.

When her hair was pinned back and her face was lightly powered, she went down to the kitchen to begin taking the food from the pantry that Cooky had labelled "breakfast". With so many guests spending the night, there was rather more food than Lady Sarah expected, but she was certain that anything left over could be returned to the pantry.

The fires had been lit in each of the rooms and there was plenty of wood and coal to keep the fires burning throughout the day.

It was not long before Arwyn rose and came down to find Lady Sarah puzzling over how to use the stove. The constable soon rescued her from her confusion and demonstrated how to boil eggs, make toast, boil the large kettle and heat the cold sausages and bacon that Cooky had cooked the day before.

By the time Wilbraham, Richard, Gordon, Sylvia, Stanley, Lee, Charles, Charlotte, Derwyn, and the doctor came down, breakfast was ready and waiting in the dining room.

The meal was jovial, and even Gordon was seen to crack a smile. Lee and Stanley could not stop talking about all the sweet treats from the Christmas Day feast as they wolfed down their food.

After breakfast was finished, there was not a crumb of food left to clear away, and the kettle had to be boiled a second time to provide everyone with enough tea for the next activity of the day.

The party was led by Lady Sarah to the drawing room, where gifts were waiting to be opened by all of her guests. When Wilbraham had informed Lady Sarah of his mother's decree, the young peeress had stolen away to find the small gifts that she had leftover from the staff boxes and gifts for the people of Stickleback Hollow.

Amongst them were pieces of confectionery, wooden toys and two small penknives. It was these gifts that Charles and Charlotte received that morning and they gleefully tore into the paper-wrapped packages to discover the treasures inside.

Upon seeing the two pocket knives that Charlotte and

Charles had received, Lee and Stanley's expressions grew dark, much to the amusement of their hostess.

"Perhaps you should look in the window seat," Lady Sarah suggested with a wry smile, and then laughed as she watched the Baker boys trying to climb over each other to be the first to reach the window seat. They lifted each of the cushions in turn until they found two packages hidden there.

Lee was the first to seize them and weighed the two gifts carefully until he was sure that he had the better of the two gifts, and handed the other to his brother.

It didn't take either boy long to find their own pen knives hidden with the paper and string. Keen to test them out, the two boys rushed out of the drawing room, forgetting the rest of their gifts, in search of old newspapers to cut into strips. Charles and Charlotte barreled after the two boys, also clutching their knives.

"Would it not be wise to go after them?" Sylvia asked with concern.

"Not at all. Let them play. Those knives are not too sharp and the loss of a fingertip is a good lesson to keep stupidity at bay," Wilbraham laughed and winked at Lady Sarah's companion.

"I had hoped not to have to render medical assistance to anyone today," the doctor sighed.

"Then let us hope that the four children are careful with their new toys," Richard said dryly to his father.

"Now, what is next for our day? We have had a delicious breakfast, we have opened these wonderful gifts, and lunch is a few hours off yet," Wilbraham asked, abruptly changing the subject.

"Pattinson will need a walk, perhaps we could head towards Swallows' End and enjoy the view for a turn or two?" Lady Sarah suggested.

"With the fires burning, and no one in the house to watch for errant embers, it may be best if we waited until a little later in the day," Arwyn suggested as he eyed the fireplace with concern.

"Or perhaps the children could be put to good use and run about in the snow with the dog until they are all too tired to cause trouble," Gordon suggested grumpily.

"I will take the children for a walk with Pattinson, perhaps clearing the dining room would be a good idea, otherwise we shall have nowhere to eat lunch," Sylvia said coolly to Gordon as she brushed past him, making for the door.

Pattinson jumped to his feet as she called his name, and trotted along behind the newest edition to the household as she went in search of the children.

"Richard, Gordon, as Lady Sarah and Arwyn made the breakfast, the least we can do is clear the dining room before lunch," Jack Hales told his sons and after cajoling them to their feet, ushered them from the drawing room.

"After lunch, I may take a turn down to the village and pay a visit to Miss DeVille," Derwyn said in an off-hand manner, causing his brother to laugh.

"Go now, you want to be with the woman you love, there is no harm or rudeness in leaving now," Lady Sarah said gently. Derwyn cast a dark look at Arwyn to silence his laughter and nodded his thanks to Lady Sarah.

"I will be back before dinner," he assured the three that remained in the drawing room before he strode out of the door.

"We should play some kind of game this afternoon, something the children can enjoy," Wilbraham suggested as the door to the manor closed behind Derwyn.

"Or sit quietly in the library at cards," Arwyn

volunteered.

"We can surely do both," Lady Sarah smiled and the three lapsed into a comfortable silence. The silence was shattered by the sound of glass breaking.

"What have they done now," Lady Sarah sighed as she rose to her feet and froze as Wilbraham grabbed hold of her wrist.

"Stay here," Wilbraham whispered and looked over at Arwyn. The policeman pulled his truncheon out from under the sofa and held it heavy in his hand.

"What is going on?" Lady Sarah asked slowly.

"It would take too long to explain, but in short, there are men who want you dead, and today is the day that afforded them the best opportunity," Wilbraham explained quickly.

"And it is why you both decided to stay," Lady Sarah sighed and shook her head.

"We will not let them harm you," Arwyn assured her. Lady Sarah pulled her arm from Wilbraham's grasp and picked up her bag from the table in the corner of the drawing room.

She flicked open the clasps and reaching in, pulled

out a small pistol.

"You still have that in your purse?" Arwyn asked with exasperation.

"Yes, I once told Mr Hunter that it was a custom from India that I did not intend to give up, and I shall say the same to you," Lady Sarah replied bluntly as she moved swiftly to the bureau in the corner of the room and pulled spare powder and ammunition for her pistol out of a hidden drawer.

"Do you always expect to be in the drawing room when you require any extra shot or have to you secreted it throughout the house?" Wilbraham asked dryly.

"What kind of fool doesn't hide ammunition and powder throughout their home for the pistol they carry in their purse?" Lady Sarah said dismissively as she loaded the pistol and primed it.

"Sarah, you do realise that you are not in the wilds of India anymore?" Wilbraham asked with exasperation.

"Forgive me for believing that it was necessary after the last few years, but I am not the one hiding truncheons in the drawing room of my host," Lady Sarah replied tartly.

"I am going to investigate, make sure that it wasn't

Richard, Gordon or Jack breaking a glass in the dining room," Arwyn said slowly, wanting to be out of the argument that seemed to be brewing between Wilbraham and Lady Sarah.

The policeman did not wait for any form of response, but slipped out into the hallway and moved swiftly to the dining room. As he opened the door, he could see that the table was almost exactly as they had left it at the end of breakfast, and there was no sign of a broken glass or plate.

"Arwyn, this way," a voice hissed from the corner of the hallway, summoning the constable to the library.

Arwyn moved swiftly across the corridor, through the slight gap in the library door and Gordon shut it silently behind him.

"Why are you in here?" Arwyn frowned.

"Men broke into the kitchen, we hid in here after they went past," Richard explained.

"Why are you hiding?" Arwyn asked with confusion.

"They're armed and we are not," Gordon replied.

"And I am a doctor, my life has been spent healing people, and I do not wish to start inflicting harm now," Doctor Hales replied as he sat in one of the high-back chairs.

"Then I would suggest you lock the door until we've dealt with these men. Richard, Gordon, fire irons are good enough," Arwyn said as he picked up the cast iron fire irons and handed them to the two men.

Just as the three men reached the library door, a shot rang out from the drawing room.

~+~+~

It had not taken Sylvia long to find the children and convince them that using their penknives to strip the bark of twigs was much more fun than cutting newspaper.

The snow was still deep around the manor, so all five of the party donned thick coats before they ventured out into the cold. Pattinson bounded out of the door and head straight for the deepest snowbank, charging through the drift and leaping out of it, only to disappear beneath the crisp and white blanket again.

The children ran after the dog, chasing him through the snow and shrieking as they went. Sylvia followed them at a leisurely pace, making sure to keep an eye on where all five of her chargers were at all times.

They had not gone far from the house when Pattinson began growling. His hackles were up and his teeth bared.

Charlotte recoiled from the dog in fright, but Lee, Stanley and Sylvia all turned to look in the direction that Pattinson was facing.

Heading towards the manor was a group of eight men, all carrying heavy clubs, and a few carried guns.

Without even thinking, Sylvia pushed the children down into the snow and grabbed a handful of Pattinson's fur.

"Stay down and quiet until I say," Sylvia waned as she lay as close to the ground as she could. The rolls of snow hid them from the sight of the men approaching the house.

Sylvia kept her head down counting the seconds as they ticked by, hoping that the children and dog would all stay quiet.

After what felt like an eternity, she lifted her head and looked towards the house, just in time to see the men disappearing around the far side of the manor.

Sylvia leapt to her feet but kept hold of Pattinson.

"We have to go, now. Run to the village, find anyone we can. We need as many people as possible to come to the manor, quickly. Do you understand?" Sylvia said quickly in a hushed voice.

"What is going on? I'm frightened," Charlotte sniffed,

her eyes wide with alarm.

"You do not have anything to worry about. We are safe. Our friends in the manor may not be. We have to find help for them. Now, on your feet. We have to be strong and not cry. Run as fast as you can and don't stop until we get to the village," Sylvia said a little more gently than before.

Charlotte took a deep breath and nodded. The boys and girl climbed to their feet and set off, running as fast as they could.

Pattinson, seeing the children running, was keen to join in the fun, and as soon as Sylvia released him, he bounded off after the four of them.

Sylvia stood and glanced back at the house, wondering whether it would be better for her to let the children find help in the village, but a voice in her head told her that she should not return to the house. She lifted her skirt and set off running after the children.

The six of them were nearly at the road when they heard the gunshot. The children skidded to a halt and looked around, uncertain of what they just heard.

"Don't stop," Sylvia shouted as she ran past them. *It didn't come from the house. It came from the woods. It didn't come from the house.* She told herself over and over as she ran, knowing full well that there would be no one hunting in these woods.

She was not looking where she was going when her feet touched the road, stepping into the path of a horse and carriage.

The horse whinnied and reared, scared by the sudden appearance of the woman. Pattinson leapt onto the road beside Sylvia, barking and jumping around the frightened horse.

"What the devil is going on out here?" Thomas Egerton asked with annoyance as he opened the door of the carriage and stepped down.

"Brother!" Charles and Charlotte chorused and rushed over to him, throwing their arms around him.

"What are you two doing here?" Edward frowned as he stepped out of the carriage.

Charlotte couldn't contain her tears any longer as she saw her two older brothers.

"Miss Sylvia, you look terrified, and Lee and Stanley Baker, you are here too, what one earth is happening?" Thomas asked as he passed Charles and Charlotte to Edward.

"Is it not a tradition to go walking on Boxing Day?" Oliver asked as he too now emerged from the carriage.

"We were taking Pattinson for a walk to Swallows End. We were not far from the house when a gang of men approached the house. We ran to find help. There was a shot," Sylvia said breathlessly and looked helplessly at the three men.

"Into the carriage, driver, take them to Wilson's Inn. Tell Wilson to get them something warm to drink and we will settle the bill when we have settled things at the house," Edward said firmly as he stood up.

Thomas walked around to the back of the carriage and opened the trunk. Inside it were shotguns that were primarily used for hunting, but they were also effective against gangs of suspicious men.

"I have the feeling that by the end of the day, I will have seen more guns here in the quiet British countryside than I have ever seen in America," Oliver sighed and took the offered gun.

The carriage lurched off with Sylvia and the four children inside. Pattinson had seen the guns and refused to climb into the carriage. Instead, he was stood by the side of the road, ready to return home and fight whatever it was that was upsetting his friends.

The three men and the dog made their way quickly up the grass banking that led back to the manor. They did not utter a word to one another as they went, only hoped silently that they would not be too late when they arrived.

They approached the house from the rear and saw the kitchen window and door had been battered down using the bench that sat under the window.

Their guns loaded and primed, the men advanced slowly, but Pattinson was not waiting. He charged headlong into danger. A deep growl in his throat and sharp teeth ready to tear at the throats of anything stupid enough to threaten his mistress.

The sounds of fighting echoed into the hallway. Pattinson bounded into the drawing room and found Lady Sarah reloading her pistol as Arwyn, Wilbraham, Richard and Gordon fought hand-to-hand with seven attackers.

One of the men slipped past the four defenders, reaching Lady Sarah, a steel pipe raised high over his head.

Pattinson did not falter as he gathered all his strength, took two strides and leapt at Lady Sarah's would-be attacker.

His jaws open, he clamped his teeth down hard on the arm holding the pipe and used his body weight to knock the man over.

The man cried out in surprise and tried to shake the dog off, but Pattinson would not release the man's arm. One of the men fighting with Wilbraham had a knife in his hand.

The captain was doing his best to avoid the sharp blade, but being outnumbered was making the fight somewhat harder, and it was only a matter of time before the knife would do more than inflict a few scratches.

The man fighting with Pattinson finally made it to his feet and still trying to free his arm from the dog, stumbled backwards into Wilbraham, forcing the captain onto the blade of his attacker.

"Brother!" Thomas yelled as he, Edward and Oliver burst into the room.

Seeing that numbers had turned against them, the attackers tried to make an escape but three shotguns and the weapons of those they had attacked, as well as an extremely tenacious Akita, caused them to surrender rather than be shot in the back as they fled.

With four guns levelled at them and their weapons

thrown down, the attackers had to wait for Richard and Gordon to fetch some rope and the doctor.

The doctor arrived first and was quick to whisk Wilbraham out of the room to see to his wounds.

"Get William, the Russians," Wilbraham spluttered to his brothers as he was carried out of the room.

The rope was a few moments behind and each of the men was bound by the hands and feet.

"What do we do with them now?" Oliver asked as he looked at the men and his cousins.

"Lady Sarah, can I take Harald and ride to the village? Our carriage is waiting at Wilson's Inn with our other siblings, Sylvia and the Baker boys. I will send them home and go fetch William," Thomas said gravely as he handed his gun to Richard.

"Of course, whilst you are gone, we shall guard our prisoners," Lady Sarah replied.

"Though, if our brother does not live, there may be one less prisoner to concern ourselves with," Edward replied coldly.

Arwyn had gathered up all the weapons the attackers had brought and removed them from the room. Only the three shotguns and Lady Sarah's pistol remained to keep the prisoners in line.

"Father and Gordon will do their best, Wilbraham is in good hands," Richard whispered to Thomas as he turned to leave.

"I have no doubt in their abilities," Thomas replied, "Though I have a feeling that Wilbraham knew that this was going to happen."

"He probably did," Richard agreed solemnly.

Chapter 17

Thomas rode as fast as he could. He settled the bill with Wilson at the inn and sent his carriage with the four children and Sylvia inside it to Grangeback.

Harald was a good and strong horse. He had been ridden by Mr Hunter until he left, and though the grooms had exercised him every day, the gelding clearly needed more.

Thomas kept the powerful creature at a canter down to the village, the long stride of the big animal kicking up flurries of snow as he went. Just before he reached the road, Thomas slowed him to a walk to avoid slipping on the unseen icy patches that often hid in the ruts of the road.

When he left Stickleback Hollow, he stayed off the road as much as possible, allowing Harald to move faster than if he was lumbered by the often deadly combination of ice and cobbled road. More than one horse had slipped in the winter and broken its leg. With no hope of recovery, it was the end of the animal's life, and Thomas would not be the cause of the death of his friend's horse.

Harald switched between a trot and canter, eating up the distance between Tatton Park and Stickleback Hollow. By the time he reached the house, Harald had barely broken a sweat and he was fit enough to make the journey back to Grangeback without a problem.

William was in the study, looking over government papers when Thomas burst into the room. It did not take much for William to be convinced of the urgency of Thomas' mission, and the pair were mounted and moving before barely twenty minutes had passed.

By the time the two arrived at the manor, the doctor had finished attending to Wilbraham's wounds. Though the knife had plunged deep, it had missed the important organs and the blood had soon been stopped.

Jack Hales worried that the captain might succumb to infection if he did not keep the wound clean, but Wilbraham was not a man to spend his time lying on his back when there were things to do.

Richard, Gordon, Edward and Arwyn were guarding the prisoners in the drawing room. Lee, Stanley, Charlotte and Charles were sat in the kitchen with Sylvia, who was busy making lunch.

The doctor and Lady Sarah were stood in the hallway discussing whether their prisoners should be fed or left hungry for a few more hours.

"How is he, doctor?" Thomas asked as he came through the front door.

"As well as any man could hope to be after he has been stabbed," Jack replied with a smile, "He should recover well, as long as he rests."

"Where is he now?" William asked.

"Lying down in the library, come with me, William," Lady Sarah said as she led the MP to where his brother was supposed to be resting.

"William!" Wilbraham said with relief when he saw his brother.

Wilbraham tried to leap to his feet, but Oliver, who was sat at his shoulder, was faster and a gentle hand on the shoulder reminded him that he should not be standing quite yet.

"You are a fool," William said crossly.

"For being stabbed, or for keeping much of this affair secret?" Wilbraham asked with a grin.

"Both,"

"Then perhaps you would be good enough to confirm whether you recognise any of the men we are holding in the drawing room, and if so where from," Wilbraham replied.

William sighed and shook his head, but knew better than to argue with his brother. He walked out of the library and found Lady Sarah waiting for him.

"The drawing room is this way," she said and led him across the hall, stopping just outside the door.

"You are not coming in?" William frowned.

"No, the doctor and I will wait with your brother and cousin. Thomas will be finished with the horses soon I imagine. Sylvia has instructions to send him to the library," Lady Sarah replied and slowly made her way back across the hall.

William had an uneasy feeling in his stomach as he opened the door and stepped into the drawing room. The seven men were still sat, bound by the hands and feet, not moving or talking. Gordon, Edward, Richard and Arwyn held the four guns on the men, should they decide that escape was a good course of action.

"Brother, good to see you," Edward said without shifting his gaze.

"Are these the ones?" William asked.

"They are," Richard replied, also keeping his eyes on the prisoners.

"I see," William said slowly as he looked over each man in turn. He didn't say anything as he tried to place each man, and when he was finished, he simply said, "Thank you," then left the room.

Thomas had joined the others in the library by the time William returned to them.

"Do you recognise them?" Wilbraham asked,

"I do. They are all men that are employed by the Russian embassy. Will you now tell me what all this is about?" William requested as he sat down and fixed his gaze steadily on Wilbraham.

Wilbraham cleared his throat and explained everything that he could. Lady Sarah occasionally provided additional explanations when required, but it did not take long for the whole tale to be laid out for all those present.

"I see. Well, the two of you are even more foolish than I believe possible, but there is nothing I can do to change that. The Russian Ambassador on the other hand. I will be back before dinner, and I will bring the esteemed ambassador with me. Ensure his men are fed and watered. I fear that we can learn nothing from these men without the ambassador present," William said at the end of it.

The driver of the carriage Thomas, Edward and Oliver had taken to Stickleback Hollow was sat in the kitchen with the children, and only too glad to be of service to William.

The pair left and the carriage was soon rolling its way down the road towards the city. Several hours had passed by the time William returned. The dining room had been laid out beautifully, so perfectly that it was impossible to tell that none of the servants had been there to help.

Mrs Bosworth, Bosworth and Cooky had all returned to the house and were horrified by all that had transpired in their absence. Cooky had set to work preparing dinner for the ambassador, and Bosworth had been keen to return to his post.

Mrs Bosworth had been the only one of them brave enough to enter the room with the prisoners and had screeched insults and threats at the seven men who had dared to try and harm her mistress.

Arwyn had always known that she was a terrifying

woman, but to see the fear on the faces of the men that had been ready to meat out murder told him that Mrs Bosworth was capable of inspiring terror in the hearts of even the most jaded of men.

Lady Sarah and the doctor had both changed into more formal attire for the arrival of the ambassador.

It had not taken much convincing to get the ambassador to travel from his rooms in Chester to Grangeback. The promise of the company of a man he considered a friend and a full table was all that was required.

As the carriage lurched its way back towards Stickleback Hollow, William explained the reason behind his visit to the ambassador and without accusing him of anything.

When the carriage stopped outside Grangeback, the ambassador stepped out of the carriage first, swept up the steps and knocked hard on the door.

Bosworth opened the door and was surprised when the ambassador swept past him and walked straight over to where Lady Sarah stood.

"Carlo Pozzo di Borgo, Russian ambassador, at your service, my lady," he said formally and bowed before her,

"May I offer you my sincerest apologies for the inconvenience you have suffered today at the hands of my people. Would you be so kind as to show me to them?" the ambassador asked as he straightened up.

"Of course, this way," Lady Sarah said with an air of confusion.

Edward had been relieved of guard duty and had gone to sit with Wilbraham. This meant that Oliver, Thomas, Richard, Gordon, and Arwyn were all in the drawing room when the ambassador entered.

Upon seeming Carlo Pozzo di Borgo, the seven men stiffed and the fear that Mrs Bosworth had instilled in them paled in comparison to the terror that was now etched in every line of their bodies.

The ambassador did not waste any time with pleasantries, instead, his voice exploded from his mouth, causing even Pattinson to jump and whine.

He roared in Russian and when he had finished, the room fell into an awkward silence that was finally broken by the man that had stabbed Wilbraham.

Carlo Pozzo di Borgo listened carefully to what the man said before replying curtly in Russian.

"If it pleases the lady of the house and the policeman, set them free. They will do nothing to harm anyone of this house," the ambassador said and Lady Sarah slowly nodded her agreement. Arwyn didn't know what to say, so simply shrugged. Richard and Gordon set about untying the ropes and the men all filed out of the room, bowing in apology to Lady Sarah as they went.

"What is going on?" Thomas frowned.

"Come, dinner is ready, I am sure that the ambassador and William will explain," Lady Sarah said wearily.

Formal introductions were made as Carlo Pozzo di Borgo made his way to the dining room, and Wilbraham was helped into the room by the doctor.

When the first course had been served, the ambassador began to explain.

"We have had many problems with revolutionaries in Russia for many years. They have become increasingly problematic as of late for the Czar, and we have all vowed to put a stop to their actions. Mr Kvietkus was known to be involved with the revolution, but he was exiled from our country some time ago. When he appeared in Chester at the time I arrived, he was reported to be a threat to my life, and the woman he was searching for was reported to also pose a risk. My apologies, my lady," Carlo said sincerely.

"You are forgiven," Lady Sarah smiled.

"You are too gracious, my lady. My aide, Sergei, has always been very devoted to the Czar and Russia, but there had been rumours of late that he was more in love with gold now than country. But I had dismissed these rumours and the prattling of those who coveted his position in the embassy," the ambassador continued.

"And now?" William asked.

"From what I was told by the men in the drawing room, the rumours are now more than substantiated. Does the name Fitzwilliam mean anything to you?" Carlo asked.

"It does," Lady Sarah said stiffly.

"It seems that this Fitzwilliam has bought the soul of Sergi. He has been twisting truths and sending all manner of harm towards you, my lady. There are not enough words to apologise for all this. But I assure you, Sergei will not be allowed to carry on. You have my word," Carlo said firmly as he slammed his fist down on the table.

"Forgive me, ambassador, but when you met with

Sergei at our home, in the summer house. The way you spoke, it seems you do not yet know that Mr Kvietkus was murdered," Wilbraham said, wheezing slightly and his voice laced with pain.

"Murdered? Why would the death of a Russian peasant be of such great importance to you?" Carlo frowned.

"He worked on my father's farm. My father sent him with a message that could not be entrusted to anyone else. It involves the kidnapping of two women that we suspect Fitzwilliam is responsible for," Arwyn replied.

"I see. So Mr Kvietkus died to protect the secrets of this Fitzwilliam. Then, my new friends, I know how to make this right. Today, Fitzwilliam has lost an ally in Russia and made an enemy of not only myself, but the Czar as well," Carlo said firmly.

"You are too kind, my dear friend. Now come, regale us with your stories of the Battle of Waterloo. None here, save for myself, have heard those yarns and I could listen to them fifty times again before I die," William said as he opened another bottle of wine and passed it down the table.

Chapter 18

The ambassador was an excellent dinner guest, and even sent men to the house the following day to repair the damage that had been caused to the windows and kitchen door, as well as the damage that had been caused in the drawing room.

The household staff had returned to the sight of broken glass and learned of the break-in and a much more dramatic account of the fight that took place in the drawing room.

Edward, Thomas, William, Charlotte, Charles and Oliver had taken Wilbraham home to Tatton Park to rest, and Doctor Hales promised to visit his patient in the morning.

Arwyn returned home to find Derwyn asleep in front of the fireplace, and the policeman mused how odd it was that he had missed dinner. Instead of waking his brother to chide him, he helped Derwyn to the spare room in the police house and let him sleep.

Richard and Gordon spent the night at Grangeback, but after the excitement of the day, retired early to their beds.

Sylvia had excused herself not long after dinner, wanting to take some time to examine the events of the day without others around. She also wanted privacy whilst she tried to surmise why she had feared so much for those in Grangeback when she saw the men approaching. It had been a long time since she had allowed herself to care for anyone, and in a few short days she had been drawn into this strange household and seemed to worry for all those even loosely connected with it.

Pattinson had not left Lady Sarah's side since the intruders had left the house. He sat when she sat. He walked where she walked. There was no world in which the faithful Akita would dare to leave his mistress exposed to such danger ever again.

Lady Sarah had not been ready to retire for the night when her guests had departed. Instead, she had retreated into the brigadier's study. It was an odd bastion within the walls of the manor. It was a place for solace and thought.

When the brigadier chose to sit in there alone, it was understood that no one should disturb him. The same was now true of Lady Sarah and had been true of Mr Hunter.

It was in the study that Doctor Jack Hales found the

lady when the rest of the house had all gone to bed.

"An exciting day," the doctor said dryly as he poured out a measure of single malt scotch into two glasses.

"A day I would happily have lived without," Lady Sarah replied with a sigh as she accepted one of the glasses from the doctor.

"The bad days are there to remind us how much better the good days are, but today could have also been far worse than it was," Jack said as he sat down in the chair opposite the brigadier's desk.

Lady Sarah was sat behind the desk, with Pattinson lying beside her.

"I have begun to feel somewhat cursed," Lady Sarah said, shaking her head, "It seems no matter where I go or what I do there are people who I am a threat to. Both Fitzwilliam and John Smith seem to stop at nothing. We have prevented Fitzwilliam from harming me on this occasion, but I do not believe this is the last time we will hear the name."

"No, I think you are right in only one respect. Fitzwilliam is an enemy, but not just of yours. I believe that we will find Grace and Millie, and it will be sooner than any of us think. Fitzwilliam does not want them found, but we shall prevail. This may mean that Fitzwilliam sees you as an enemy for life, but I believe that is a burden you could shoulder with some help from your friends. John Smith, she is another matter altogether. Since the brigadier left though, she does not seem to have any axe to grind with you. It may be that whatever business she had with your parents is now settled," the doctor replied between sips of whisky,

"Do you think he will be home soon?" Lady Sarah asked hopefully.

"The brigadier or Mr Hunter?" the doctor asked with a wry smile.

"Either. Both," Sarah said with a deep sigh.

"You are not alone in missing them, but I will admit the hurt for you is far greater than it is for any of us," the doctor said gently.

"The brigadier has been called away by duty, and it has been a joy to have the Baker boys in the house whilst their mother is away with him, but it is beginning to feel like he will never come back, that we will simply receive a telegram saying he will never return. What would happen to us all then?" Sarah asked with tears in her eyes.

"Then you would carry on with the grace and poise

with which you have handled everything that has been thrown at you so far in your short life. You are strong and independent. You have friends about you that would do lay down their lives for you. As evidenced by the events of today. But George would not leave you so suddenly. He would not wish you to bear another loss on his behalf," Jack said warmly.

Lady Sarah looked up from the desk to meet the kind gaze of the doctor and could not help but feel a little better.

"And what of Mr Hunter?" Sarah asked helplessly.

"He is young, selfish and given to flights of folly," the doctor shrugged, "But he is not stupid. He will realise what he has left behind and that it cannot be found anywhere else in the world, let alone the North of England. He will come home and when he does, you can decide whether to forgive him or whether there are more deserving men. No one, especially the brigadier, will think less of you for wanting to be respected and loved."

"Life does not get any easier, does it?" Lady Sarah chuckled as she finished the last of the whisky.

"No, my dear, it does not."

Chapter 19

The investigation into the murder of Mr Kvietkus was closed on 27th December. There was no need for it to remain open once Carlo Pozzo di Borgo named his aide, Sergei, as the man responsible for the crime.

Constable Clowes arrived in Stickleback Hollow a few hours after the ambassador had told the police everything to inform Arwyn.

Derwyn and Arwyn listened with great amusement to every detail of the denouncement of Sergei to his arrest. He had been dragged out of the ambassador's rooms and thrown into the street before he was collected by the police.

Arwyn had repaid Constable Clowes by regaling him with the tale of the Boxing Day attack at Grangeback and the ambassador's part in the whole affair.

Derwyn listened to both stories with amazement and cursed himself for having departed not long before the men had appeared at the house.

Arwyn thought it was strange his brother had not come across the men on his journey down to the village, but he did not comment on it.

On the 28th December, a newspaper was delivered to Grangeback by the ambassador with the headline

Revolutionaries Assassinate Murdering Bureaucrat

"It seems that Sergei has met an untimely end," Carlo said as he handed over the newspaper to Lady Sarah. She read the article aloud, detailing the men that were believed to be involved, and the man who had committed the assassination stating clearly that "it has been done to avenge brother Kvietkus and all those that have suffered at the hands of our Czar"

"Then the matter is settled," the doctor said with a wave of his hand.

"It is indeed, I would like to thank you for your help in the resolution of all this by inviting you all to dine with me this evening," the ambassador said.

There was no refusing such a kind offer. The dinner was not a simple affair, and more of a ball, where Lady Sarah was introduced to any and everyone of any note by the ambassador, who judiciously told of the great service that had been done for both England and Russia by the young lady and her companions.

Arwyn declined to attend the dinner and instead spent the evening writing to his father. He detailed everything that had happened since the first letter that his father had sent and finished it with:

In short, father, the information that you sent with S Kvietkus has been lost due to his murder. Please arrange another delivery.

Your loving son

Arwyn

Chapter 20

On 31st December a New Years' Eve Ball was held at Tatton Park. It was a smaller gathering of people than the Christmas Eve Ball as it was being held not just to celebrate New Years' Eve, but also to say goodbye to Wilbraham.

"My orders arrived this morning. I am to report for duty in India," Wilbraham explained when he greeted Lady Sarah.

"Then may your journey be blessed. I must admit I do miss it," Lady Sarah sighed.

"If I could take you with me, I would gladly have the company, but I fear there would be gossip, and you are needed here," Wilbraham tried to console the lady.

"You are right, but for the tongues of gossip and the pressures of responsibility," Sarah laughed.

"As it will be sometime before I have the pleasure of your company again, may I claim your dance card for this evening?" Wilbraham asked with a bow.

"Of course, it will save me from rebuffing the advances of lesser men," Lady Sarah chuckled.

"Ah, I fear that I will have to wait for a dance or two. I believe that you may wish to prepare yourself for a moment before you turn around," Wilbraham said slowly.

Lady Sarah took a deep breath and turned around slowly. Stood in the doorway to the ballroom stood Mr Alexander Hunter. He was dressed for the occasion in a top hat and tails. His white shirt was crisply ironed, and Lady Sarah suspected that Mrs Bosworth had a hand in his attire.

He looked uncomfortable and nervous as he scanned the room, looking for Lady Sarah. When his eyes finally landed on her, he felt his breath catch in his throat.

He had not thought it possible, but she was even more beautiful than she had been when he last saw her. He slowly made his way across the ballroom, praying that she would not turn away from him.

"Mr Hunter, what a surprise," Lady Sarah said trying to keep her heart from exploding out of her chest.

"Yes, I know that my arrival might be somewhat unexpected, but I received a letter from Arwyn, and that coupled with the wisdom of a friend I shared the road with for a time, it made me realise I had made a terrible mistake," Mr Hunter began to explain.

"I see," Lady Sarah said, turning her head to look at Wilbraham, who was grinning at the pair.

"I know that it would be almost too much to ask of you, but could you ever forgive me for leaving?" Alex asked with hope in his voice.

Lady Sarah studied the face of the groundskeeper as he stood before her. He was still the same man that she loved, his face still made her heart leap at the sight of it. His voice still soothed her, but there was still pain etched upon her heart.

"You were the first man that I ever loved, and I still do love you. So for the sake of the love I have for you, I do forgive you. However, for the sake of my heart and keeping it from further pain, we cannot go back to what we were," Lady Sarah said sadly.

"Your forgiveness is more than I could have hoped for. I know that for now, you cannot trust me, you cannot love me as you once did. But I will not stop loving you or trying to protect you," Mr Hunter replied firmly.

"If you will excuse me, Mr Hunter, Wilbraham has claimed my hand for the evening. I do not wish to keep him waiting any longer," Lady Sarah said, trying to keep her voice as even as possible. She turned back to Wilbraham, who took her hand and whisked her away to the dance floor to keep her from breaking down into tears.

"Excuse me, sir, might I have your name?" an American voice asked from behind Mr Hunter.

"Alexander Hunter, and you are?" Alex asked defensively.

"Mr Oliver Henry Brown, cousin of the Egertons," Oliver replied coolly.

"I see, you are the gentleman that has been pursuing Lady Sarah," Alex replied through slightly gritted teeth.

"Not yet, but I do intend to. You are the man that broke her heart, and even though you shattered it, she still loves you. It's not hard to see that from across a crowded room," Oliver shrugged.

"She may have loved me once, but not anymore. That doesn't mean I intend to stop trying to win her back," Alex said with a slight smile as he watched her dance.

"Then may the best man win," Oliver said smugly before he turned and walked away from the groundskeeper.

"He will," Alex said under his breath.

Lady Sarah tried to push aside the shock of seeing Mr

Hunter suddenly return and focus solely on Wilbraham.

"You will be missed, you know," Lady Sarah said suddenly as the pair waltzed around the floor.

"I know. I will miss you as well," Wilbraham smiled.

"Your wound hasn't healed fully, has it?" Sarah asked with concern.

"It has healed enough," Wilbraham tried to dismiss the lady's worries.

"You are still favouring your side. It has not healed. Please be careful. I do not wish to lose another friend," Lady Sarah replied sternly.

"I will do all I can to stay alive, I promise," Wilbraham assured her.

"Then I should ensure that I say my farewells to you tonight. There are things that we often leave unsaid, and I have learned that they are often the most important. You have been one of the dearest friends I have made in England. You have been stabbed for my sake. You were the one to bring Mr Hunter back to me, at least in part. There are no words that I can say to express how grateful I am to have you in my life. So if this is to be our last meeting in this life, I would have you know that I love you as dearly as any sister could love any brother," Lady Sarah said with a sad smile on her face.

"Thank you, sweet sister," Wilbraham smiled back, "You are quite possibly the most extraordinary woman I have ever met. Do not lose that and become another giggling idiot at court. There are enough of those to fill all of England."

"I will do my best, dear brother," Lady Sarah agreed. As the night flew by and the hands of time counted down to the New Year, Lady Sarah wished her friends goodnight and left to return home.

"Sarah, wait," Alex called out as he followed her down the steps outside of the great house.

"What?" Sarah asked as she stopped but did not turn around.

"I know you are angry and hurt. I know that you have forgiven but don't trust me, but I have to know whether you might ever love and trust me again, and there is only one way I can think of to know for certain. If you cannot love and trust me again, I will not trouble you again," Alex blurted out.

"How much have you been drinking?" Sarah

frowned.

"Nothing. I have not drunk a single drop of alcohol since I left Stickleback Hollow," Alex replied with surprise.

"Then why say all this now?" Lady Sarah demanded.

"Because this is a time of new beginnings," Alex said simply.

"And how can you know for certain?" Lady Sarah asked with exasperation.

"Like this," Alex said as he gently turned her to face him, tilted her chin upwards and lightly kissed her lips. Lady Sarah closed her eyes and kissed him back, far more fiercely than either of them expected. When they finally broke apart, Lady Sarah was the first to speak.

"Does that help?" she asked, her arms still wrapped about his neck.

"It does," Alex replied with a smile.

"Then I will say goodnight, Mr Hunter," Lady Sarah grinned as stepped back and slowly drew her hands down his face.

"Goodnight, my lady, and Happy New Year."

~*~*~

Lady Sarah is determined to solve a mystery that has been plaguing her for a year. Can she put the pieces together and bring her friends home safely, or will this mystery prove too much for her?

Spring in Stickleback Hollow, Book 11 in the Mysteries of Stickleback Hollow is waiting for you now.

~*~*~

Thank you for reading **Christmas in Stickleback Hollow**. I hope you enjoyed it! Want to read more about the adventures of Lady Sarah? An exclusive story about them is available for free for all my newsletter subscribers. Visit https://mailchi.mp/cea2332e3102/cs-woolley-newsletter to sign up and get access to it, and a whole heap of other exclusive content, offers and contests.

~*~*~

Love **Christmas in Stickleback Hollow**? Then go back to beginning and see where it all started in **A Thief in Stickleback Hollow**. *She can't believe her parents are gone. But the noblewoman's arrival in England has exposed a mysterious conspiracy that stretches across the British Empire.*

~*~*~

Want to help a reader out? Review are crucial when it comes to helping readers choose their next book and you can help them by leaving just a few sentences about this book as a review. It doesn't have to be anything fancy, just what you liked about the book and who you think might like to read it. **Visit** https://mybook.to/ChristmasinStickleback **to leave a review.**

If you don't have time to leave a review or don't feel confident writing one, recommending a book to your family, friends and co-workers can help them choose their next book, so feel free to spread the word.

Historical Note

The Welsh Sheepdog is not the same things a Welsh Collie. In fact, a Welsh Collie is a crossbreed between a Welsh Sheepdog and a Border Collie. Welsh Sheepdogs are bred as herding dogs and are very active and intelligent, so they need a lot of exercise and can work whilst not under direct human control. They are used mostly for herding sheep, but also for cattle, horses, goats, and even pigs.

There have been people living in Lithuania for millenia, but the modern country of Lithuania has only existed for a relatively short time. In the 9th to 11th Century the Lithuanian peoples were subject to viking raids and had to pay tribute to the kings of Denmark. In the 12th Century the Lithuanians were the ones raiding Russian territory and they even began raiding with the Polish peoples.

The Grand Duchy of Lithuania didn't exist until the 13th Century. In the 16th Century Lithuania and Poland former a union that lasted until 1795. From 1795 to 1834, Russia controlled much of Lithuania. In 1830 to 31, the November Uprising took place. The uprising is also known as the Cadet Revolution and the Polish-Russian War. It began in Warsaw on 29th November 1830 when Polish army cadets revolted (the names for it are all very imaginative as you can see). People in Lithuania, Belarus and even the Ukraine all joined the revolution. However, the Russian military eventually crushed the uprising. As a result Poland lost its autonomy and became absorbed into the Russian Empire.

The Lithuanian uprising was only of a minor importance to the war, but in it the young Countess Emilia Plater and a group of other women disguised themselves and engaged in guerilla warfare in the frontier provinces. It had little effect other than to allow the Russians to crush local uprisings and subjugate the population.

Victorian diplomacy had wide reaching effects and consequences. For those of you that have read "What Became of Henry Cartwright?" you will already by aware of the impact that failed diplomacy and the development of gunboat diplomacy had not only on China but Japan as well. There were diplomats with embassies within Victorian society, and often they were of high social standing. Immigration was a very different issue to the ones that we see today. The majority of migrants to England were Irish, though there were also Eastern European migrants as well.

Internal migration in Britain also increased dramatically. There was a net movement of people away from the countryside and rural areas to the urban and industrial landscapes of the cities. Britain had an open door policy when it came to migration until 1905 when restrictions were first put in place. Though not all migrants received a warm welcome, British Victorian society was not xenophobic and no form of blanket hostility to migrants existed. Most of the negative attitudes that migrants encountered were due to poor experiences with certain migrant groups.

The Irish potato famine between 1845 and 1851 was the the major cause of the mass migration of Irish settlers to England.

Carlo Pozzo di Borgo was he Russian ambassador to the United Kingdom of Great Britain and Ireland from 1835 until 1839. A Corsican by birth, he was considered a traitor to his country because of his opposition to Napoleon Bonaparte. He fought at the Battle of Waterloo and was singled-out in Wellington's post-battle dispatch. He was an extremely interesting man with a strong sense of duty. It is for this reason that he is not the villain of the piece, and instead that it was a fictional aide inside the embassy that was behind the subterfuge.

The Vicar of St John's Knutsford was quite possibly the hardest fact I have had to root out in all of my research so far. I found the name of Robert Clowes in a book that listed clergy of England in the early Victorian period. I believe that he was still the vicar of St. John's when this book takes place, but if I misread the book and he had been moved on, I do apologise - as far as the occupants of my books are concerned, I was right and that is enough for the story.

The Christmas Tree was brought to England in the 1790s by

Queen Charlotte (Queen Victoria's mother), but the Christmas tree was popularised by Prince Albert. Large trees had gifts put under them, but most people had small trees that sat on their tables.

Christmas was not really celebrated until 1848 when a drawing of Queen Victoria and Prince Albert appeared in the Illustrated London News showing them and their family celebrating Christmas around a decorated Christmas tree. This began the transformation of the Christmas season from one of the least celebrated festivals to the most celebrated festival by the end of the century.

You may have noticed that the Christmas Cracker was missing from the Christmas celebrations in Stickleback Hollow, and that is because it was not invented until 1848 (it was a very big year for Christmas). It was invented by a confectioner, Tom Smith, who was inspired by the French giving sugared almonds wrapped in paper. So he created a paper cracker that was filled with sweets so it could easily be pulled apart for the treats inside.

Christmas gifts were originally given at New Year, but moved to Christmas, and to begin with they were sweets, nuts, fruits, and handmade gifts for people. However, they became shop bought and larger as time went by and were soon moved under the Christmas tree. The small gifts were used to decorate the Christmas trees.

So in their celebration of Christmas, Stickleback Hollow was certainly ahead of its time, but only by a few decades.

"when fear and guilt were making people acutely conscious of lower-class suffering, the role of the philanthropist took on an importance, even a necessity, which called for the rhetoric of heroism" *Houghton 320*.

Philanthropists within Victorian society were extremely well thought of. There were many notable philanthropists in Victorian Britain, which is arguably why Scrooge's transformation in Charles Dickens' A Christmas Carol was so important. The philanthropists in the story that came calling on Scrooge to collect donation for the poor and needy on Christmas Eve are an indication about how important it was for those who were fortunate to have an abundance to give to those who did not.

For Lady Sarah, blessed with two fortunes from her parents and the fortune that the brigadier is set to settle upon her, philanthropy is something that cannot be avoided. Fortunately, she is of a generous spirit that fits well with being a great benefactor.

Boxing Day was traditionally a day off for servants, and the day when they received a special Christmas box from their masters. The servants would also go home on Boxing Day to give Christmas boxes to their families.

Gifts were wrapped in paper and string, like packages. They did not have the same level of brightly coloured papers that we use to day and sticky tape did not exist either.

The history of the Pen Knife is an interesting one, and highlights why the name pocket knife is quite a misnomer. The pen knife was a sharp knife that originally did not fold, but was carried around in order to cut quills into new nibs, hence the name pen knife. Larger folding knives were known as clasp knifes. However, as time went by, the term pen knife became widely used for both. The folding knife was safer to transport and was also required to open newspapers in the mid-1800s.

For those that remember the introduction of the Egertons in All Hallows' Eve in Stickleback Hollow may remember that Wilbraham Egerton Junior died in 1841. So his journey to India is the last one that he will make. He has said his goodbyes to his friends and family, and though it pains me to say goodbye to Wilbraham, his brief time upon this earth is up and we must move forward without him.

About the Series
Mysteries abound

When her parents die from fever, Lady Sarah Montgomery Baird Watson-Wentworth has to leave India, a land she was born and raised in, and travel to England for the first time. Finding it almost impossible to adjust to London society, Sarah flees to the county of Cheshire and the country estate of Grangeback that borders the village of Stickleback Hollow. A place filled with oddballs, eccentrics and more suspicious characters than you can shake a stick at, Sarah feels more at home in the sleepy little village than she ever did in the big city, however, even sleepy little villages have mysteries that must be solved.

Set in Victorian England, the Mysteries of Stickleback Hollow follows the crime solving efforts of Constable Arwyn Evans, Mr. Alexander Hunter and Lady Sarah Montgomery Baird Watson-Wentworth. From theft to murder, supernatural occurrences and missing people, Stickleback Hollow is a magical place filled with oddballs, outcasts, rogues, eccentrics and ragamuffins.

Preview from the next book

Spring in Stickleback Hollow

Lady Sarah is determined to solve a mystery that has been plaguing her for a year. Can she put the pieces together and bring her friends home safely, or will this mystery prove too much for her?

Spring has brought a time of new hope to Stickleback Hollow along with the news from Wales that Grace and Millie have been found. But the reasons for their kidnapping are still a mystery, and it is up to Lady Sarah to not only solve that mystery, but the two young women home safely.

After a year of searching, the two women seem so close to returning home, but the kidnappers will stop at nothing to keep the women from being found.

Can the heroic heiress prevail or will her friends be lost forever?

Grab **Spring in Stickleback Hollow** now!

Also by the Same Author

The Mysteries of Stickleback Hollow

A Thief in Stickleback Hollow
All Hallows' Eve in Stickleback Hollow
Mr Daniel Cooper of Stickleback Hollow
The Day the Circus came to Stickleback Hollow
A Bonfire Surprise in Stickleback Hollow
Tinker, Tailor, Soldier, Die
What Became of Henry Cartwright
The March of the Berry Pickers
The Advent of Stickleback Hollow
Christmas in Stickleback Hollow
Spring in Stickleback Hollow
Lady de Mandeville in Stickleback Hollow
A Day Trip to Brighton
12 Days of Christmas in Stickleback Hollow
Easter in Stickleback Hollow

Chronicles of Celadmore

Rising Empire: Part 1
Rising Empire: Part 2
Rising Empire: Part 3
Rising Empire Trilogy
Shroud of Darkness
Lady of Fire
End of Days
Shroud of Darkness Trilogy

The Children of Ribe

FATE
WAR
WIFRITH
DOUBT
SKÅNE
SHIPWRECKED
FEAR
HOME

The Arm Rings of Yngvar Collection
TREASON
MURDER
SEDITION
STRIFE
SUSPICION
ALLEGIANCE
DECEIT
REGICIDE

The Bergkonge Collection
BETRAYAL
JOTUNHEIMR
ALFHEIMR
NILFHEIMR
SVARTALFHEIMR
MUSPELLHEIMR
VALHALLA
RAGNAROK
The Rise of the Völvur

The Children of Snotingas

WYRD
HILD

<u>Nicolette Mace: The Raven Siren</u>

Medusa

Siren's Call

Shadow

A Shot in the Dark

From Out of the Ashes

The Murder of Michael Hollingsworth

The Case of Mrs Weldon

Hunting the Priest Killer

Beginnings

Manhunt

A Friend in Need

Gangster's Paradise

Ring of Fire

Return of McGregor

Murder in the First

Sabrina

Last Train Home

Til death do us part

How do you solve a problem like Siren?

Siren, Fred and Harry Saga

Filling the Afterlife from the Underworld: Volume 1

Filling the Afterlife from the Underworld: Volume 2

Filling the Afterlife from the Underworld: Volume 3

Filling the Afterlife from the Underworld: Volume 4

Poetry

Standing by the Watchtower: Volume 1

Standing by the Watchtower: Volume 2

Indie Visible: Vol. 1

<u>Shakespeare Simplified</u>

The Merchant of Venice

The Merchant of Venice Key Stage 3 Workbook

The Merchant of Venice Key Stage 3 Teacher's Guide

Further information on these titles can be found at
mightierthanthesworduk.com

Books Adapted by C. S. Woolley for Foxton Books

Level 1 400 Headwords

The Wizard of Oz by L. Frank Baum

The Adventures of Huckleberry Finn by Mark Twain

The Adventure of the Speckled Band by Arthur Conan Doyle

Anne of Green Gables by L. Maud Montgomery

Dracula by Bram Stoker

The Prisoner of Zenda by Anthony Hope

The Lost World by Arthur Conan Doyle

The Little Prince by Antonie de Saint-Exupéry

A Little Princess by Frances Hodges Burnett

The Secret Garden by Frances Hodges Burnett

Level 2 600 Headwords

Moby Dick by Herman Melville

Gulliver's Travels by Jonathan Swift

Alice in Wonderland by Lewis Carroll

Sleepy Hollow by Washington Irving

Treasure Island by Robert Louis Stevenson

Around the World in Eighty Days by Jules Verne

Robinson Crusoe by Daniel Defoe

Beauty and the Beast by Gabrielle-Suzanne Barbot de Villeneuve

Heidi by Johanna Spyri

The Jungle Book by Rudyard Kipling

Level 3 900 Headwords

The Three Musketeers by Alexandre Dumas

Pocahontas by Charles Dudley Warner

Oliver Twist by Charles Dickens

Frankenstein by Mary Shelly

Journey to the Centre of the Earth by Jules Verne

Call of the Wild by Jack London

Level 4 1300 Headwords

The Count of Monte Cristo by Alexandre Dumas

The Merchant of Venice by William Shakespeare

The Railway Children by Edith Nesbit

Jane Eyre by Charlotte Bronte

The Mysteries in Stickleback Hollow: Christmas in Stickleback Hollow

<table>
<tr><td>

Level 5 1700 Headwords

The Thirty-Nine Steps by John Buchan

David Copperfield by Charles Dickens

Great Expectations by Charles Dickens

Twenty Thousand Leagues Under the

Sea by Jules Verne

</td><td>

Level 6 2300 Headwords

Kidnapped by Robert Louis Stevenson

The Mysterious Island by Jules Verne

Other

11 Plus Flash Cards

</td></tr>
</table>

About the Author

I was born in Macclesfield, Cheshire, UK, and raised in the nearby town of Wilmslow. From an early age I discovered I had a flair and passion for writing.

I began writing at the age of 7 and was first published in 2010. I currently live with my partner, Matt, and our two cats in Christchurch, New Zealand.

As an avid horsewoman and gamer, I also have a passion for singing, dancing, the theatre, and my garden.

Facebook: https://www.facebook.com/AuthorC.S.Woolley

Instagram: https://www.instagram.com/thecswoolley

Website: http://.mightierthanthesworduk.com

For access to exclusive content, contests and freebies, sign up for my newsletter here

https://mailchi.mp/cea2332e3102/cs-woolley-newsletter.

Acknowledgments

Writing can be an extremely lonely profession at times, but thankfully I never have to go through any of the pressures alone. My wonderful Matthew has been a source of constant support to me during all of my writing endeavours since we first met. I couldn't ask for a more fitting partner to share my life or love with.

Writing is not something I stumbled into either, my mother, Helen, took me, and my sisters, to the library every weekend when we were young to get different books, and I always maxed out the number of books I could get. Not only did she encourage me to read, but to write as well. To say I have been writing stories and poetry since I was 7 is not an exaggeration and the development of my writing career is due in no small part to her.

My mother-in-law, Lesley, has also been a source of unflinching and unwavering support, something I could not do without.

To Laura and Sam, who have read and offered opinions, death threats and encouragement on my early drafts, you are true treasures. Amy, you too are worth your weight and more in gold for all your love and support.

It may seem that writers only function alone, but I am blessed to be part of an amazing community of authors whom I know that I have helped push me to even greater heights and success. So to Quinn Ward, Donna Higton, Charlene Perry, Scarlett Braden Moss, Bryan Cohen, Chez Churton, Eliza Green, John Beresford, Rich Cook, Robert Scanlon, Jen Lassalle, Cathy MacRae, Ariella Zoella, and Helen Blenkinsop, my dear friends, thank you.

And finally, to you, dear reader, without you there would be no books, no series, no career. I want to thank you for all the time that you spend reading my work, reviewing it, sharing it with your friends and family. Without you there would be nothing. Thank you from the bottom of my heart. If you haven't already signed up for my newsletter, please do. Newsletter subscribers get access to an exclusive section of my website that is filled with additional content, free stories and contests that are not available anywhere else. To sign up, just visit https://mailchi.mp/cea2332e3102/cs-woolley-newsletter.

Until we meet again in my next book, thank you and adieu.